The Perverse Utopia

Exploring its Fiction, Philosophy

and Social History

by

ALAN GREENHALGH

RB

Rossendale Books

About the author

Alan Greenhalgh has undergraduate degrees in psychology, allied health and radiography, and postgraduate degrees in humanities, religious studies, Japanese language and society, and environmental consultancy.

After an initial interest in German (he was taught the language by an ex-World War 2 Nazi interrogator), he studied Japanese and trained as a teacher and lecturer. He has taught at various UK and Japanese educational establishments, including St. Andrew's University, Japan - a country he lived in for ten years.

For two years, he presented the highly successful The Mystery Zone, a paranormal radio programme for Salford City Radio.

He is married and currently lives in Manchester, England where he divides his time between teaching and writing.

Published by Rossendale Books
11 Mowgrain View, Bacup,
Rossendale, Lancashire
OL13 8EJ
England

http://www.rossendalebooks.co.uk

Published in paperback 2012

Historical, Political & Philosophical Essays

ISBN 978-1-906801-70-0

To my mother and father

CONTENTS

Preface

In this book I explore the relationship between man and society in Utopia. I will examine seemingly disparate themes such as harmony, freedom and its expression, conflict, the Russian Revolution and Stalin, robots, homosexual rights to marriage and religion; for all of these topics relate to Utopia, or the attempt to realize it. For example, in the case of Arab political history and religion, one may at first question the legitimacy of its relationship to Utopian themes. However the Arab version of the Utopian ideology was translated by Muhammad through religion into its secular narrative - the aim being the achievement of that perfect society we call Utopia.

I will review a small selection of the Utopian books available; books which highlight man's search for Utopia through literature, philosophy and political systems. Also reviewed will be the thematic opponent of Utopia: dystopia - the reality of man's failure to achieve his ideal society.

Thomas More's *Utopia*, which is set somewhere in the New World, is a good starting point to investigate the relationship between the individual and society. It is a book that combines humour, interest and wit. Apart from More's *Utopia*, I must of course mention Yevgeny Zamyatin's futuristic *We*, the famous *Walden Two* by B. F. Skinner, and of course, William Morris's socialist, *News From Nowhere*. These books will be among those I will sometimes refer to in this work.

The book will explore certain issues relevant not only to today but to the later part of the 21st century and to the 22nd century as well; a new era whose beginning is already upon us. Each chapter will have its own theme and will be comprised of mini essay-like component parts, each relating to that particular theme, and will discuss such matters as harmony, freedom and its expression, conflict, trade, language, robots, religion, fallen Utopias, control and democracy.

Some of the contemporary issues featured in this book have been covered in Utopian literature; others we face today: the death penalty, controlling the population, same-sex marriage, the function of religion, and the conflict between man and authority. Of course these issues must also be faced well into the 21st century and probably beyond. The underlying theme of each topic however, is the conflict, which has always existed, between man and the society that gave birth to him.

Introduction

Nobody would pretend for a moment that Thomas More's *Utopia* was a serious political tract. Paul Turner says as much in the introduction to a reprint of More's book, when he says that the book combines humour, interest and wit.[1] Apart from More's *Utopia*, I must mention Yevgeny Zamyatin's *We*, from which some tentative ideas came into being from the spirit of the work, especially the futuristic aspect of the novel. George Orwell's *1984* and Aldous Huxley's *Brave New World* are of a similar mould, although given the content of the novels, dystopia rather than Utopia would be a more fitting description of them.

The Perverse Utopia: Exploring its Fiction, Philosophy, and Social History is a different animal altogether. It is neither fictional nor political, but more philosophical. It makes the reader think about certain issues relevant not only to today but to the 21st century, and indeed future centuries. Each chapter discusses a variety of matters such as the concept of harmony, freedom and its expression, conflict, trade, language, robots, religion, fallen Utopias, control and democracy. Even topics on Arab political history and religion feature, and although the reader may at first question the legitimacy of such writings in the present book, I hope the fact that the Arab world has its own version of the Utopian narrative will become clear and consequently justify its presence to the reader.

One thing is indubitable: the world has changed and is still changing at a truly breathless pace, and we as human beings are helping to effect these changes. Some of the contemporary issues that we face today: the death penalty in America, same-sex marriage, the function of religion and the conflict between man and authority are very emotive, but we must face them unswervingly because as we are thrown headlong into 21st century uncertainty, these problems we face collectively as a society could be aggravated by further issues of the technological sort like the advancing technology of robotics - once restricted to the realm of science fiction, but which is now a rapidly developing field of reality - and the moral sort, like control of the population. And do not let us hide our heads in the sand; the horrendous reality of control of the people arrived long ago. Mumford says as much in his magnanimous work, *The City in History* (1961):

> 'Processing' has now become the chief form of metropolitan control...the monopoly of [this] power and knowledge that was first established in the citadel has come back, in a highly magnified form, in the final stages of metropolitan culture. In the end every aspect of life must be brought under control: controlled weather, controlled movement, controlled association, controlled production, controlled prices, controlled fantasy, controlled ideas.[2]

So what is the aim of *The Perverse Utopia: Exploring its Fiction, Philosophy, and Social History*? The essays contained in the book are primarily there to bring about a response on the part of the reader to think for himself about the multiplicity of potential futures awaiting us. I also hope, however, that the book is informative with regards to the part Western politics is playing in directing us (or not) along a possible Utopian trajectory.

The hopefully informative essays indicate the potential of man and state to reach the Utopian ideal. We can only realize this potential ourselves. We are alone, like primitive amoeba in this park called earth, and the park is there for us to play in and enjoy; not to destroy. Man is actually his own future and it is a future we must ourselves choose. As Sartre fatefully declares:

> ...man is in consequence forlorn, for he cannot find
> anything to depend upon either within or outside

> himself...We are left alone without excuse. That is what I mean when I say that man is condemned to be free. Condemned, because he did not create himself, yet is nevertheless at liberty, and from the moment that he is thrown into this world he is responsible for everything he does.[3]

I hope of course, as we all do, that we employ love and reason to the mighty task ahead of us - that of forging a secure future - and not use the differences that exist between us to annihilate ourselves. We must remember that we can be our own Gods. We can re-invent ourselves time and again into something better. We *can* be *'ManGod.'*

This book is a playground of ideas; it is not ideology, for it presents a vision not dogma.

Unlike Thomas More's *Utopia* which is set somewhere in the 'New World,' we know exactly where the Utopian spirit of *The Perverse Utopia: Exploring its Fiction, Philosophy, and Social History* is: it is our earth in the 21st century, and indeed beyond. Let us all pray, not to God, but to the wisdom in man for the chance of a beautiful future. We have a blank canvass before us because the future belongs not to God, but to us; the world is eternally ours to renew.

Notes

[1] Thomas More, *Utopia*, trans. Paul Turner (London: Penguin, 1965) 7.
[2] Lewis Mumford, *The City in History: Its Origins, Its Transformations, and Its Prospects* (New York: Harcourt, Brace & World, Inc., 1961) 542.
[3] Walter Kaufmann, *Existentialism from Dostoevsky to Sartre* (Rev. ed. New York: Meridian, 1989) 353.

CHAPTER 1

Real and Imaginary Utopian Systems

Global Village - Amoeba Park

However much we question the feasibility of the Utopian ideal, we cannot escape the fact that plausible Utopias can only exist within the range of already defined and existing parameters; parameters based on the current political landscape. It is rather difficult to conceive of Utopia emerging as something totally new, something never before seen on the globe. It seems much more tenable that when Utopia finally comes - as I believe it will do - that it will be a hybrid political system. Its internal dynamic may well be eclectic: borrowing something from democracy as well as something from communism. And when Utopia does finally come, will it be led by some dynamic leader - a Utopian Stalin (if one can conceive of such a persona), or an Obama or a Cameron? Or will the leadership be a kind of Utopian cooperative, with a committee rather than a single leader? We simply do not know; but whoever, or whatever it is, their ideology, their 'Utopistical'[1] philosophy - to borrow Immanuel Wallerstein's terminology - will undoubtedly have tenets in common with all previously existing and contemporaneous political philosophies. As Wallerstein acutely observes:

> [Revolutionaries]...discover that, as individuals and regimes, they are constrained by the structures of the world-system to behave in certain ways and within certain parameters or else they lose all capacity to be important actors in the world-system. And so they bend their intentions to the realities, if not sooner, then later.[2]

In discussing the French Revolution as a starting point, Wallerstein goes on to say that political systems re-invent themselves or are simply transposed into something quite new; and that, most significant of all, the process is a normal one. I would agree; but in talking of the emergence of Utopian systems, something extra would be required for a society to match mankind's true aspirations. It would be a system, as I said before, which might be a curious political/philosophical hybrid; but in addition, it might contain something unique which would engender a historical system without a history: that is, time would stop. By "time" I mean the political, social and historical chronology of events which are studied by politicians, sociologists and other policy makers for their predictive validity. Francis Fukuyama has disseminated a related theory in his best seller, *The End of History and the Last Man*. Fukuyama believes that history has already come to an end because of a dissatisfaction with the world-wide legitimacy of liberal democracy. In many ways, liberal democracy is just a very successful political system which, in a Darwinian sort of way, has superseded all other previous (that is historical), political systems. This system must itself be superseded by something new and partially unique. Although he does not predict what will come to replace it, Fukuyama does assert the end of the present system when he argues that: "liberal democracy may constitute the end point of mankind's ideological evolution" and the "final form of human government," and as such constitutes the "end of history."[3] History, I assert, will only end when *all* government-based political systems - whatever their nature may be - vanish from the globe.

But I do not think the advent of the new Utopia will be akin to a revolution. Revolutions and the social and political circumstances which lead to them are of a different nature altogether. In the case of the Russian Revolution for example, Bolshevik insurrection was not instigated so much by political intellectuals as by voluble individuals who seized the opportunity - in a time of national hunger and vanquishing of the body politic through war - to offer a vision of a political system which would solve the kind of problems whose response by the former autocratic rule was one of impotence.[4]

The new world will probably emerge through the gradual disintegration of existing political and government structures - and it may not be pleasant. Wallerstein firmly believes that:

> We are living in the transition from our existing world-system, the capitalist world-economy, to another world-system or systems. We do know that the period of transition will be a very difficult one for all who live in it. It will be difficult for the powerful; it will be difficult for ordinary people.[5]

Do we have any inkling as to what the nature of the changes might be? Wallerstein proclaims the eventual disintegration of capitalism as an effective historical system. Reasons are manifold. All over the world major corporations have destroyed the landscape and the atmosphere in their greedy drive to increase profit margins. And safe disposal of waste is an expensive business; so much so that it can often be in their fiscal interest to dispose of waste illegally, thereby adding to the already polluted globe. For the more honest companies who care about the environment, the reward is an ever-increasing financial burden.[6] As profit margins decrease there is less capital to be had, and therefore more opportunity for economic stagnation. Note that Fukuyama, aware of some of the negative connotations of the term 'capitalism', distances himself somewhat from the term and uses 'free-market economics.'

But something else is contributing to the sociomoralism of consumer America and the European economic model. Although capitalism has superseded other systems like the now obsolete Soviet model, in terms of being able to produce an unending range of products to enhance our life-style, many citizens - especially those who have access to these products - seem to be asking themselves if they really need them.

We only need to look at the Arab world to witness the long-standing rejection of the capitalist model; though it is worth noting that even if the model had been accepted, it would never have got off the ground. In Syria and Iraq, for example, during the post-war years, although potential industries did exist, neither the capital existed to develop those industries, nor the workforce (with the required skills) existed to work in them.[7] Even now however, Islam is one of the strongest rivals of Capitalism, and has taken the place of the obsolete Soviet model in challenging the capitalist direction of history.

For Fukuyama, liberal democracy has developed in line with, and gives free rein to, the free market economy. However, although capitalism is the strongest economic model now, will it be so in the future? Will Lenin's observation that, "Capitalism had bought time for itself..." prove to be true?[8]

Notes

[1] Immanuel Wallerstein, *Utopistics: Or, Historical Choices of the Twenty-first Century* (New York: The New Press, 1998) 1.
[2] Wallerstein 12.
[3] Francis Fukuyama, *The End of History and the Last Man*, (New York: Avon, 1993) xi.
[4] Wallerstein 25.
[5] Wallerstein 35.
[6] Wallerstein 44-45.

[7] William R. Polk, *The Arab World Today*, (London: Harvard U. Press) 1991, 273.
[8] Fukuyama 99.

Individual Liberty: Various Social Models

Burkean conservatism versus radical democracy

It is quite inadequate to discuss the concept of individual liberty among historical social models without explicating two major philosophical works which lie at the centre of any discussion of Utopia. The political theories put forward in Edmund Burke's *Reflections on the Revolution in France* and *The Rights of Man* by Thomas Paine, lie at opposite ends of the political spectrum.[1] Paine's work was actually a response to Burke's; his accusation being Burke "pities the plumage, but forgets the dying Bird;" a reference to Burke's uncompassionate treatment of the oppressed in the French Revolution.[2]

Reflections postulates what has become known as Burkean conservatism despite the fact that traces of it have also become evident in liberal thought; while Paine's work extols the virtues of liberty through radical democracy and natural rights, along with what has become known as the social contract. Each work shapes our definition of what form individuality and personal liberty should take. Both of these are central to any conceptions of Utopia.

Burke - who claimed to love "regulated liberty"[3] and whose wisdom and authority seem to originate, "...beyond the grave..."[4] - believed sincerely that, "Men must have a certain fund of moderation to qualify them for freedom...The liberty I mean is social freedom...[and is] secured by the equality of Restraint..."[5] In Burke's model, liberty could only mean individuality, or separateness from the whole, something which could only detract from the well-being of society. It was the church and government who secured liberty through a hierarchical structure, where rights were socially determined.

For Burke, revolution meant the end of such traditional institutions.[6]

According to Thomas Paine, liberty took a more discernable form, the idea that man is a social entity being relegated to second place. Of most importance was the concept that all men had natural political and economic rights which took precedence over any societal obligations as citizens.[7] In Paine's radical democratic world, man only agrees to take part in society if society in turn guarantees his individual rights along with ensuring a safe and just living environment.[8] In other words, a society of liberty is maintained only if government fulfils its part of the social contract.[9] Burke also had his own form of the social contract between citizen and state[10] - a timeless one referred to as a "partnership."[11]

According to Paine, men have the opportunity to realize themselves fully, aided by the guarantee of equal rights, and assisted by negating the influence of the privileged classes - particularly those constituting the government, the church and royalty. For Paine's society to be secured, men only require reason to understand fundamental principles along with the wish to be free.[12]

Liberalism

John Stuart Mill advocated a kind of social reform that challenged the society of the time by seeking freedom from the physical and intellectual chains that held men in their place.[13] The liberalism put forward by Mill in *On Liberty*, became inextricably linked with nationalist tendencies, the tenets of the political movement gradually expanding to incorporate more varied ways to bring about liberty for the common man. Although at first it might seem that Paine and Mill have much in common, what differentiates Mill is firstly his discarding of the social contract and the concept of the natural rights of man, and secondly the desire to bring about revolutionary change without revolution; in other words, to use the processes inherent in the parliamentary system to renovate the social structure and thereby bring about liberty.[14] In addition, education was seen as a stepping stone to this liberty because it enabled man to achieve his full self-worth by providing insight into what was ultimately best for him.[15] Mill believed that liberty does not exist in the societal system, but in man himself. It is almost as if Paine were saying that one was born with natural rights, while Mill believed one had to earn them.

The aims of Mill were the same as those of Paine, but the methodology behind securing and maintaining those aims took a more conservative path - a trait which ultimately undermined the efficaciousness of the movement. Both society and the individual were dependent on each other. Society was expected to withstand the current of social mobility through the emergence of individual freedom of expression, while the individual was obligated; not obligated to society, but to himself: to realize his full potential, not in a selfish way, but in a manner which would be also useful to society.[16] This idea, unquestionably borrowed from the English law reformer Jeremy Bentham, was interpreted by factory owners, as lending credence to the notion that employees and others among the population not possessed of disposable capital should remain at the bottom end of the social scale. Although this was not quite what Mill had in mind when he defined his version of liberty for all, he did redefine Bentham's formulaic "the greatest good of the greatest number" into a new concept where the value of the state equals the value of the individuals constituting it, the latter being measured by the degree of personal liberty enjoyed in the society.[17]

Perhaps it is inadequate to try and look at the question of how liberty was maintained by Mill's social model, for liberty did not remain in the original form that Mill conceived it;

rather it gave birth to a plethora of offshoots, among them socialism, to which we now turn.[18]

Socialism

The arrival of socialism came with the advent of the industrial revolution in the 19th century. Socialists decided that the liberals had failed in their attempt to create a society of liberty and equality; the socialists wanted a society where the citizen was firmly part of the community. Some socialists like Robert Owen did manage to secure liberty for his workforce through his "...model industrial community..."[19]

What socialists wanted was a world where liberty was not dependent upon personal wealth and ownership of property.[20] Engels, for example, sought liberty for the masses through, "...new economic conditions..."[21]

Differing from socialism in its means of acquiring liberty, the philosophy of anarchy sought more rebellious pathways. Anarchist philosophy allows man to realize individual liberty (group liberty in the case of Proudhon) through the dissolution of authority.[22] Anarchists secure a *natural* society by instinctive and revolutionary rejection of the majority who control the existing state of affairs.[23]

Conclusion

All the social models have their own merits and demerits. Irrespective of the philosophies they postulate, what they try to achieve is the correct balance between the role of man and the role of society; a balance which is an important Utopian concern. The result of these social models is that liberty is defined and perpetuated in different ways. For example, according to Paine's philosophy, society functions only when men are free and consent to its continuation.[24] In one way, this selfishness of the individual contrasts sharply with the loyalty of the "...civil social man..."[25] in Burke's society - the citizen who knows that "...Moderation is a Virtue..."[26] For John Stuart Mill, liberty was breaking away from the excesses of rationalism and seeking, "...the poetry in human beings..."[27] On the other hand, liberty, according to the socialist definition, is really about using society to control wealth and thereby bring quality to men's lives rather than quantity to the economist. Finally, anarchists seek to give back to individuals the freedom and the state of non-dependency, which governments had taken, thereby fulfilling *their* own moralistic obligations.[28]

Notes

[1] Eric Foner, Introduction, *Rights of Man* By Thomas Paine, (New York: Penguin, 1985) 15.
[2] Bamber Gascoigne, *Encyclopedia of Britain* (Basingstoke: Macmillan, 1993) 475.
[3] Edmund Burke, *Reflections on the Revolution in France* Ed. Conor Cruise O' Brien, (London: Penguin, 1986) 89.
[4] Thomas Paine, *Rights of Man* Ed. Eric Foner, (New York: Penguin, 1985) 42.
[5] Burke 14-15.
[6] Conor Cruise O'Brien, Introduction. *Reflections on the Revolution in France* By Edmund Burke, (London: Penguin, 1986) 10.
[7] Foner 17-18.
[8] Foner 11.
[9] Paine 70.
[10] Burke 135, 194.
[11] Burke 150.
[12] Paine 45.
[13] John Stuart Mill, *On Liberty* Ed. Currin V. Shields, (New Jersey: Prentice Hall, 1956) 24, 39, 42.
[14] Mill 91.

[15] Mill 13, 71, 76, 82, 92.
[16] Mill 14.
[17] Gascoigne 60.
[18] Gascoigne 421.
[19] Gascoigne 471-2.
[20] Burke 140-1.
[21] Lewis S. Feuer, *Marx & Engels: Basic Writings on Politics & Philosophy* "The German Ideology," (N.p.: n.p., n.d.) 70, 107.
[22] George Woodcock, *Anarchism* (New York: The New American Library, 1962) 20.
[23] Woodcock 9, 12, 23, 33-4.
[24] Paine 67, 144.
[25] Burke 150.
[26] Burke 15.
[27] Gascoigne 421.
[28] Woodcock 28.

The Individual and Society

According to Lewis Mumford in his outstanding book, *The City in History*, harmony was an element which the ancient city apparently lacked. Indeed this view is readily suggested when Mumford talks of the ancient city as "...exist[ing] in a state of tension...that moves periodically toward[s] a crisis or climax." Mumford confirms this idea of tension as opposed to harmony, when he defines urban living in terms of, "...the confrontation and struggle of man with man...."[1]

According to Robert Redfield, man's evolution has resulted in the creation of *urban man*: an individual whose identity is cast and further shaped by the evolution of city culture. According to Mumford, this evolving of the identity of urban man is the city's reason for existing. The relationship between the individual and society serves two purposes: firstly, man is defined by the city; secondly the resultant uniform identity of the city rejuvenates itself by re-inventing the architecture and social norms of the urban village. In this sense, harmony is disrupted because the tension of the city is never completely dissipated; merely limited by the fashions of the time. The process continues until the emergence of urban man's unceasing new identity reinvigorates the potential staleness creeping into the city dynamic. Robert Redfield's comment that, "The remaking of man was the work of the city" suggests the relationship between the individual and society is not static, but is a relationship based on continuous fluxation, each combining to serve and transform the other.[2]

Indeed man and the community may be seen as two independent forces battling each other and culminating in the individual's inner growth. This is exemplified in Sophocles' play, *Antigone*, where the heroine, Antigone, is forced to choose between the command of the monarch and the duty and devotion she feels towards the religious customs relating to the burial of her brother.[3]

Harmony, and the conflict between Antigone and the legal obligations of the society imprison her. Indeed any notion of harmony proves disastrous in the context of the play. In an attempt at maintaining it, the old nobles, as does Ismene, treat Kreon's ruling as "a law" thereby endorsing Antigone's death sentence.[4] For Antigone, it is only through death that harmony can be attained.[5] Haimon, emphasizes that laws must be harmonious with the sentiment of the people. Kreon, whose speech is the focus of the play, chooses to ignore both this and the importance of love, and brings about civil discord.[6]

Conflict between man and his society must be presented dramatically through dialogue; classical tradition dictates it; as Glaucon says to Adeimantus in *The Republic*, "I'm afraid I'm talking too theatrically."[7] When we see the characters in the play facing this conflict, we witness the tragic possibilities of our own fate.

That is why *dialogue* is the medium used to full effect in *The Republic* and *Antigone*, and differentiates both dramas from the narrative of Mumford. Mumford merely details the development and unavoidable conflict of man in his community; Plato and Sophocles, on the other hand, permit one to actually *feel* it through the display of tension set up by the predicaments of the characters. Mumford talks *about* dialogue but does not use it as a stratagem for understanding the emotions of those who dwell within the city. Just as Kreon uses dialogue to uphold authority, Plato uses it to challenge authority.[8] This show of opposition through language is tolerated, even valued as part of the normal functioning of Greek society; its side effect being the displacement of harmony through the opposition to uniformity.

In ancient Greece, harmony was inextricably linked to the city and the physical body. Harmony of the body was expressed by the colossal statues of the polis; in stone, the spirit of the new age became incarnate.[9] Harmony in the city was realized as the ancient villages slowly gave way to the new urban order of the polis. Further, with the advent of the free citizen came the harmony and justice of equality. This notion of equality was further echoed in the similarity of the rich and poor abodes of Athens.[10] In addition, doctors and crafts-people earned the same salary; free citizens and slaves also worked side by side.

However, in the case of the Hellenic city, how this measure of aesthetic harmony was achieved by the Greek citizen, can be readily understood. As most inhabitants of the polis had slaves to take care of everyday housework, the Athenian citizen had the leisure time to appreciate the beauty surrounding him.[11] This new *ideal* society, ignoring the plight of the slave, while having the leisure to become a free thinker and question authority, can be exemplified no better than in the figure of Sophocles. At a time when the sanctity of the gods was giving way to the power of the citizen, the right to make one's own choices was, for Sophocles, paramount despite possible opposition from the polis.

This "golden mean" celebrating the relationship between the individual of Athenian society and the rest of the polis, can be seen in the way the average citizen had the opportunity to undertake different occupations - from actor to legislator, in the law courts - necessary for the day to day functioning of the city. Indeed the polis became the centre of all existence: an harmonious, if not ideal focus of work, leisure, art, music, politics and love; "For a while, city and citizen were one...."[12]

Glimpses of the ideal city may be seen in the Hellenistic age, although creativeness and further development was stifled by new gods: music and literature.[13]

Literature, in particular the writings of Plato, was the medium best suited to expressing this obsession with Utopia. Not satisfied with the artistic and cultural gains of society, Plato highlights the distinctions between the polis as it could be: the dreamy ideal; and the city as it actually was. Although he expressed this disillusionment most eloquently, the ideas put forward in *The Republic* do not translate into an acceptable democracy by anyone's standards.

According to Aristotle, it was the town-planner Hippodamos, who had the talent to actualize Utopia. Hippodamos' strength lay in translating an aesthetic consciousness into a practical plan, while remaining acutely aware that architectural design and social order are two faces of the same coin. In this respect architecture could be used to exploit the desire for the ideal.[14] If a new urban order was to complement the change in the pattern of the city, how would it be achieved in its most idealized form? It was Hippodamus who answered with the conviction that the people should be separated into artisans, husbandmen and armed defenders of the state. As for property, there would also be a division of sacred, public and private land. This mathematical predilection for three continues in *The Republic*: Plato subdivides members of his society into three classes, and also divides the personality into three elements.[15]

The polis in Plato's day did have many admirable qualities but Plato's disenchantment with the current achievements of his day was reproduced in *The Laws* as well as in *The Republic*. It is somewhat ironic that in *The Laws*, Plato regresses to the ancient agricultural village - a precursor to the polis - praising its "tranquil life."[16]

Plato's tribute to harmony is certainly a contradiction because as Mumford says, "...between 480 and 430 B.C....the polis for the first time assumed an ideal form that *distinguished* it from all earlier villages and cities...."[17]

One cannot read *The City in History*, *The Republic* and *Antigone* and isolate man from the setting in which he appears. One must take into account the fact that man is a social and political animal,[18] for "...only in the city can a full cast of characters for the human drama be assembled...."[19]

Even the superficial witness to this "human drama" will see the gross contradictions in Plato's *The Republic*; contradictions that lead to injustice. Plato acknowledges the individuality of men, but in a way that reinforces the view that they should remain isolated in the paths and roles chosen for them by family tradition and fate. This view is obviously inconsistent with the facts as Mumford describes them.[20] According to Plato, for harmony of the ideal state to flourish, the fisherman should remain a fisherman, and the craftsman and peasant should have no pretensions about becoming anything except the trades that define them. Such is the nature of freedom on a leash.[21]

For Plato, it is not man's individuality that is of importance but society. Indeed Plato was ready to immolate the freedom of the individual for the sake of the freedom and functioning of the city.[22] However, in proposing to surrender the freedom of the individual to the functioning of the polis, Plato was denying its citizens the potential to re-invent themselves and subsequently shape the future of men into something other than a static absolute. Plato's biggest oversight was that by denying freedom, he was depriving people of the necessary beneficial learning effects of chaos, confusion, tension and failure, for it is only against these things that mankind can measure its success in overcoming them.[23]

Plato's Utopia fails as a dream city where the individual and society are supposed to coexist in perfect harmony. Indeed Plato thinks harmony can be learnt.[24] Plato was advocating the prohibition of aesthetic pursuits, marriage and even luxury in *The Republic*; indeed his advocating of the ideal degenerated into a kind of perverse monologue. It is an ideal for discussion, not action. After all, who could legitimately defend the contradictions of slavery, injustice, Grecian unity through war, and the downright inequalities so evident in Plato's Utopia? The charm of *The Republic* as a piece of intellectual writing therefore remains damned by the unceasing tension between Plato's perverse ideal and reality as it exists in the drama and dilemmas of the city.

The most ironic thing about this endless search for harmony and Utopia, despite Plato's writings, is that Athenian life actually grasped it, if only momentarily: Mumford hints at this almost perfect state of affairs when he states that, "The role of the polis was admirable: every part of the city had come to life in the person of the citizen." However, "...it could not remain transfixed into a static image of perfection."[25] The suggestion then is that the polis did achieve Utopia but could not hold onto it. Adeimantus' words are quite poignant here: "We are like people searching for something they have in their hands all the time...we haven't seen it but have been making perfect fools of ourselves."[26]

And finally, when Mumford states that, "Growth and death will take their toll," doesn't he really mean that *change* is the eradicator of any gains made in the accomplishment of the ideal city?[27]

Notes

[1] Lewis Mumford, *The City in History: Its Origins, Its Transformations, and Its Prospects* (New York: Harcourt, Brace & World, Inc., 1961) 114-115.
[2] qtd. in Mumford 4: 116.

[3] Sophocles, *Antigone*, trans. Richard Emil Braun. Ed. William Arrowsmith (New York: Oxford UP, 1973) 39-41, 222-3, 1020.
[4] Sophocles 73-81.
[5] Sophocles 1047-51.
[6] Sophocles, 228-9, 882, 839-850.
[7] Plato, *The Republic*, trans. Desmond Lee. Ed. Betty Radice Rev. ed (London: Penguin, 1987) 3.413b.
[8] Sophocles 224-30; 798-824; 934-41.
[9] Plato 4.420c.
[10] Mumford 160-163.
[11] Mumford 160-165.
[12] Mumford 167-168.
[13] Plato 4.424c.
[14] Mumford 172.
[15] Mumford 172-173; Plato 4.435b-c, 441-c, 442c, 443d-e, 444b.
[16] Mumford 173.
[17] Mumford 159.
[18] Lyle Smith, *Evolution of Human Culture: Western Civilization* Ms. Hux 540. Rev. ed. (California State. U., Dominguez Hills, 1996) 10.
[19] Mumford 116.
[20] Mumford 167.
[21] Mumford 174; Plato 3.415-c, 4.420e-421c, 423d, 433, 434-b, 443c.
[22] Plato 3.413c-e, 4.420b.
[23] Mumford 177.
[24] Plato 3.413e.
[25] Mumford 169-170.
[26] Plato 4.432d-e.
[27] Mumford 170.

Freedom and its Expression

At the outset, it is important to realize that freedom and the loss of it takes many forms. In Mumford, More and Shakespeare, one can see examples of the gaining of freedom, the loss of it, the nature of its manifestation, and the way it has developed through history, from ancient Greece, through to the Middle Ages and later Renaissance, and finally to the Baroque period, right up to the present day.

In the medieval city, it was the church which was the controlling influence on life and community. As the medieval era was drawing to a close, economic interests became more and more prominent bringing about freedom from religious constraints. Although Mumford compares the periodic medieval barbarism - and the ultimate loss of freedom in the guise of man's inhumanity to man - to the barbarism of today, freedom for the medieval town dweller became a reality.[1] It was the church which set the process in motion through its religious doctrines. But the same fervour which ensured that the serf could be a free citizen was also evident in the church's materialism. The religious buildings of Christianity met no limit in their expense and extravagance, a policy once seen in the Athens of Pericles.[2] In essence, freedom was achieved through the church in the medieval city, but at the cost of financial wisdom.

However, many of the changes medieval life brought were freedom orientated: the Christian city meant freedom expressed by adjusting the balance of power, changing the law and property rights, the abolition of slavery, and employment opportunities as well as economic justice for both rich and poor.

In addition, skilled workers in the medieval period reclaimed their freedom from a society based on a graded social hierarchy, as a result of the itinerant nature of the work and the fact that the tools of the trade were their own. In a word: mobility and the open road meant freedom in more ways than one.[3]

Whatever gains the medieval city offered in terms of civic liberty, the chance of freedom exemplified by the religious life was smothered when money and power became more important, just as in the Greek city.[4]

Venice, the epitome of the Renaissance city, was the place where, via architectural planning, freedom was defined in its most magnanimous way, though the means was often perverse. The city planning in Venice brought freedom through utility, within the context of a "new urban order."[5] Here, *utility* is the key word with regards to freedom; for what better way to define freedom of the city than by utility for the whole populace, along with growth, re-adaptation, change and unity?[6]

Despite the apparent merits of Venice, our image of the Renaissance is wrong. Freedom was not the objective: architecture, art and the advancement of the intellect within the context of European culture was.[7] The term *Renaissance* is a misnomer: there was no re-birth because there were no major changes in the social order. There was only a modification of the medieval city.[8]

But there were more serious problems of a political nature beside an inept use of terminology. The political inequity thinly disguised as a formal system, allowed the rulers to behave like the totalitarian leaders of the 20th and 21st centuries. One can compare the Atomic Energy Commission, the National Security Council and the Central Intelligence Agency to the political order of Renaissance Venice. The Renaissance city may be projected onto the modern age in terms of subduing freedom. Indeed, "...the suppression of truth and the elimination of any alternative to the accepted policy..."[9] is the suppression of freedom in its most grotesque form.

In talking of academic freedom, it is possible to draw comparisons with the Renaissance suppression of freedom - following the Black Death in the 14th century - with the suppression of academic freedom in the 20th century.[10]

What is interesting is that the Venetian public did not object to the totalitarianism of the governing body because though they lost any sense of political freedom, they gained benefits - or perhaps one should use the term *rights*, in terms of public services, employment and spectacular festivals. And anyway, even if the citizens did not have freedom *in* the city, they gained freedom *from* it through the dematerialization of the city wall or boundary; a necessity in the ancient Greek citadel.[11] But if one looks at city planning in Renaissance Florence - a "free city" - one may see the freedom of Italian design at the expense of human comforts.[12]

In Thomas More's *Utopia*, freedom is expressed in terms of "...both an economy of abundance and a fullness of leisure...."[13] It is the city of the likes of "Amaurote" which offers freedom in the form of:

> ...its desire for equality, in its effort to spread both goods and leisure, in its conversion of work into a form of play, and both into a means of sustaining the mind...Here...is the social city of the future...toward...[which] the great cities of the world have still a long way to go.[14]

This so-called freedom however, is of the regulated kind. For example, a person may not leave his district without a passport.[15] In addition, freedom in More's *Utopia* has become standardized like the costume and manners, into a form of "collective control" albeit without the suppression of freedom and ultimate totalitarianism of Renaissance Venice or the 20th century. More's sense of social freedom is based, "...upon the absence of variety and choice..."[16]

More's own idea of freedom was in allowing for the expansion of the mind. In discussing More's work, Mumford again draws comparisons with modern-day Europe when he talks of propaganda and warfare in *Utopia* and asks rhetorically, "Is this, again, Eutopia?"[17]

More's *Utopia* however, does advocate freedom, but his ideology cannot escape the influence of barbaric ideas like the perpetuation of slavery.[18] Even when freedom is apparent it takes odd forms like liberal and excessive leisure time as everybody only needs to work six hours a day; or freedom of the road: vagrancy in non-Utopian parlance,[19] or even freedom to take a person's life, not through murder but perfectly "honourable" and legal euthanasia.[20]

We can see Shakespearean freedom in *The Tempest*, although one should be aware that beneath the "masque" of the play lies a "...principle of order..."[21] This order is a microcosm of Elizabethan society; an order which rules at the expense of freedom.[22] As Lorie Jerrell Leininger notes,[23] this is apparent, for example, in Prospero's - as head of the family - reply to his daughter, where sexism is the way freedom is restrained, "What! I say, My foot my tutor?"[24]

One cannot change the hierarchical order of society. Freedom's antithesis, slavery, is also apparent throughout the play (Brower's "slavery-freedom continuity.")[25] Caliban sings of freedom while drunk, and boasts of the servility that will end.[26] But when he does free himself temporarily from his "tyrant master" the result is abuse and mockery from Trinculo.[27] Caliban is born a slave and so must remain one; Ariel on the other hand is in a sense free even though he is bound, for what could be freer than "...the fluid elements of water and air..."[28] And Caliban is never promised freedom by Prospero, while Ariel is.[29]

All the characters save Prospero and his daughter experience slavery or imprisonment, before they are set free in Act V. For Ferdinand, love is a desired loss of freedom,[30] and Gonzalo's notion of freedom is actually his Utopia.[31]

Although Prospero has the power to enslave and release those under him, as in the case of Ariel, Caliban and even his daughter Miranda - in terms of his blessing her romantic association with Ferdinand - Prospero himself is imprisoned as the epilogue explicitly states, "...release me from my bands [bonds]...Let your indulgence set me free."[32]

In conclusion, a measure of freedom did come with the destruction of the walled-in medieval city.[33] But freedom was not to last. The shift of power aided by the introduction of gunpowder in the 14th century, also caused the previously democratic and free cities to decline. This shift in the balance of power even resulted in a certain loss of freedom and security for the previously mobile craftsman.[34]

Once we get past the misleading image generated by the word *Renaissance* we can see the real nature of freedom as it existed in Italy.[35] There are many instances worthy of examination. In times of war, for instance, the municipalities of Italy employed professional soldiers, who would later become masters of the people, resulting in a loss of civic freedom.[36] Italian cities even gave up their freedom. Only the Swiss and the Dutch maintained civic liberty. National identity took precedence over civic liberty due to a transference of political power to the capital.[37] We can also see a loss of autonomy with the advent of the bureaucratic regime and its necessary office buildings.[38]

Neither Venice nor Amaurote succeeded in escaping the flaws which defined them.[39] And of the Middle Ages, little in the way of a positive note can be seen. Indeed once again we can compare the tyrants of the past with those of the present day. For example, in the Middle Ages, he who could fund the military, could rule and become supreme despot. Even today, however, our freedom is threatened by such "...totalitarian and quasi-totalitarian imitators..."[40]

The unshackling of mankind in its diverse forms, from the constraints history imposes on it, in the form of both tyrant and society, is never accomplished easily; rather it must be fought for and won.

But the roles of liberty are also fluid and reversible. As Bernard Knox says, "...free men can act and think like slaves and slaves rise superior in intelligence or emotion to their masters."[41] Or to put it another way, is not the hollow master the unwitting servant of the slave?

Notes

[1] Lewis Mumford, *The City in History: Its Origins, Its Transformations, and Its Prospects* (New York: Harcourt, Brace & World, Inc., 1961) 316.
[2] Mumford 317.
[3] Mumford 338.
[4] Mumford 320-321.
[5] Mumford 321.
[6] Mumford 322.
[7] Mumford 345.
[8] Mumford 348.
[9] Mumford 324.
[10] Mumford 346.
[11] Mumford 324.
[12] Mumford 349, 352.
[13] Mumford 326.
[14] Mumford 326.
[15] Thomas More, *Utopia*, trans. Paul Turner (London: Penguin, 1965) 84.

[16] Mumford 327.
[17] Mumford 327.
[18] Mumford 327.
[19] More 47.
[20] More 102.
[21] Robert Langbaum, introduction, *The Tempest* by William Shakespeare (New York: Signet, 1987) xxiii.
[22] Langbaum xxvi.
[23] Lorie Jerrell Leininger, "The Miranda Trap: Sexism and Racism in Shakespeare's *The Tempest*," ed. Robert Langbaum (New York: Signet, 1987) 209.
[24] William Shakespeare, *The Tempest*, ed. Robert Langbaum (New York: Signet, 1987) I.ii.469-70.
[25] Reuben A. Brower, "The Mirror of Analogy: *The Tempest*," ed. Robert Langbaum (New York: Signet, 1987) 184.
[26] Shakespeare II.ii.186-95.
[27] Shakespeare III.ii.26-35.
[28] Langbaum xxv.
[29] Shakespeare I.ii.245-46, V.i.240-42.
[30] Shakespeare III.i.39-42, III.i.65-67, III.i.86-88.
[31] Shakespeare II.i.150-61.
[32] Shakespeare V.i.9-20.
[33] Mumford 348.
[34] Mumford 356.
[35] Mumford 347.
[36] Mumford 352.
[37] Mumford 355.
[38] Mumford 354.
[39] Mumford 328.
[40] Mumford 361.
[41] Bernard Knox, "*The Tempest* and the Ancient Comic Tradition," ed. Robert Langbaum (New York: Signet, 1987) 169.

Progress versus Freedom

Progress is a term encapsulating a plethora of connotations. It would be fallacious to argue that progress always means freedom and harmony, because human history has shown this not to be so. And our image of progress is a distorted one if we equate it with evolution as an upward spiral whose tip is graced by some Utopian ideal.

Of course showing the folly of progress within the context of the Utopian dream has been a common theme in fiction, and follows a long literary tradition including George Orwell's *1984*,[1] Aldous Huxley's *Brave New World* and B. F. Skinner's *Walden Two.*[2] Zamyatin's *We*, of course pre-dates all of these works, and yet in spirit, strangely post-dates them. *We* is a frightening literary experience unable to escape its postmodern time frame. It is frightening because we can see the shadows of Zamyatin's future in "our" present. Interestingly, Joseph Wood Krutch points out, "...that whereas Plato's *Republic* and More's *Utopia* are noble absurdities, [B. F. Skinner's] *Walden Two* is an ignoble one..."[3] Does not *We* also fall into the ignoble category? At any rate, what all these dystopian stories warn of, if we really look, is a future we might well inherit.

In the *Invisible Man* Ralph Ellison does not see progress as a single path upwards or towards the future, but as a process which travels in all directions. Ellison's anti-hero beautifully highlights his own version of the manner and movement behind his place in human history:

> Not only could you travel upward toward success but you could travel downward as well; up and down, in retreat as well as in advance, crabways and crossways and around in a circle, meeting your old selves coming and going and perhaps all at the same time.[4]

For Ellison, fiction is a way to show us Utopia as an unattainable mark distanced from reality. Fiction is the best means of showing us how poorly we have evolved as human beings because although writers and styles, like the generations and periods that give birth to them change, racism, inequality and bigotry have remained the same. Ellison's use of the medium of fiction seems an almost desperate hope to achieve ends the democratic political arena has so far denied us.[5]

Could the main character in the book be Ellison's catharsis? Does not the invisible man seek to become the Utopian man? At any rate, the invisible man seems to think his freedom is tied to his identity.[6] His identity however, seems shaped by those who hold his future in their hands. The employers to which the hero sends his letters of reference seem to have the power of those who are not mortal. As the invisible man observes: "But the letter brought no reply. Nor any more than a prayer unanswered by God, was it returned."[7] This existentialist pattern of thought where the distance between the common man and his creator-employer seems infinite and appears to parallel the "Benefactor" in *We*. Although D-503 believes the ancients were misguided by "...their irrational unknown God...who gave them nothing but eternal tormented searching,"[8] he fails to see that control is hidden behind the order of the "table of hours."

There seems to be no dividing line between God as creator and God as employer in either *We* or in the *Invisible Man*. And there can be no real freedom because the individual only functions to serve "we," the majority, who in turn only function in the city to serve the Benefactor. The citizens of "OneState" still believe that the Benefactor serves "them." Those who believe this mistakenly think progress has been achieved. Ironically, harmony is a by-product because there is nothing to break the circle of functional dependency between the creator and the citizens.

Progress and the reality of history

Before twentieth century politics and dystopian fiction clouded the issue, progress meant a different thing all together. From the 1700s on, aristocrats defined progress as financial success through industrialization of the city. And subsequently forsaking the place where one's fortune was made, aided by the security and pleasure of profit to the serenity of country life, was the criteria of success. This was because although civilization was the root of all progress, it was also the basis of a multitude of complexities.

It was the fleeing of these complexities, made possible through wealth, which drove the rich out of the town and into the country.[9] The European ideal became situated in the life of the country. The country was sanctuary. It meant being away from the stress, smog and suppression of city life. In essence, the country was an escape from progress.

With the march of industry came the loss of freedom both for the wealthier members of society and for the poor. For the rich, escape was possible: financial profit virtually guaranteed it. For the poor however, there was no escape, no freedom, and no harmony; the necessities of function overrode such concerns.[10]

Even in the eighteenth century, the city of London had its fair share of progress of the industrial kind, which was accompanied by its fair share of smog. And in the following century, what free and unused land was available in the town was seized by developers and industrialists to be used to dump refuse and slag.[11] But it was not only London where progress "took control," Manchester as we shall see, also developed from a market town into an industrial dystopia.

The Mancunian miracle

Nowhere can the economic evolution of man, as well as the ironies of so-called social progress, be seen better than in the historical portrait of Manchester. Manchester, which lies on the east bank of the River Irwell, is an old town in northwest England. When the Roman invaders came to Britain they built a Roman fort there in AD 79 and named the city "Mancunium," and the people who reside there are still known as Mancunians.

Progress there began when Flemish weavers came in the 14th century to what was then a market town. It was cotton which started the initial transformation of Manchester into a great industrial metropolis at the beginning of the 18th century.[12]

In many ways, the geographical location of Manchester was advantageous. The early cotton mills needed water to power the spinning machinery and rivers were never far away. And when the appearance of the first steam engines came, there were plentiful supplies of coal in the Midlands.

Through the mechanization of the cotton industry, aided by such people as John Kay, James Hargreaves and Samuel Crompton, Manchester soon became a great metropolis. But there was a downside. It was in the unending work schedule of the smoke emitting factories of Manchester, that people lost their freedom. It is no accident that the small park where my grandfather used to take me to play in Salford, a metropolitan borough of Manchester, was named "Chimney Pot Park."

Productivity could only be achieved by a mechanization of factories and people;[13] and though this downside of Manchester is rooted firmly in the past, the circumstances and the processes which begot this state of affairs could easily be transplanted to Zamyatin's OneState.[14] There was less freedom for the factory workers in Manchester than for the citizens of Elizabethan life or in the imagined cities of Plato or Thomas More.

Just as political insurrection was not tolerated in Shakespeare's time, neither was it in Manchester. When the Liverpool and Manchester railway opened in 1830, the ironies of economic progress took on a dehumanizing form. The revolt that eventually surged forth - known as the "Peterloo massacre," which occurred even before the complete industrialization of the city, can be compared with the revolt of the Harlem community in the *Invisible Man* when the people are angered by the racism and their low standard of living, and turn to rioting as a solution. In Manchester, a crowd of around 60,000 people gathered peacefully - unlike the mob in Ellison's book - to protest the economic recession and high food prices following the Napoleonic Wars. Despite the peacefulness of the crowd and the fact that they were unarmed, the magistrates ordered troops to remove the gathering, in the process killing around eleven people and injuring about five hundred.[15]

And just like Ellison's anti-hero who comes as a stranger to Harlem and tries to shape the lives of the black community by peaceful, political means, and ends up having his own life shaped, so did Friedrich Engels, one of the leading political advocates of 19th century communism, have the same experience when he came to Manchester:

> ...it was in Manchester's mills that the political ideas of the young Engels were formed. His father owned a textile factory in Germany and had a share of one in Manchester, where the young Engels was sent to work (1842-4). His experience of the human misery...caused him to write, when only 24, a classic of political sociology, *The Condition of the Working Class in England.*[16]

The escape to suburbia

In response to the rise of the industrial community, came the romantic suburb. The romantic suburb was an attempt to answer the chaos and dissatisfaction of the big city. It created harmony, and freedom from disease, crime, prostitution and other social evils. This in itself was progress, but it was of an unfair kind as it did not uplift the poor working classes still left behind in the metropolis.[17] The suburb then was an attempt at progress and harmony. It was also an escape; but of a form worthy of disdain. The people who fled to the suburban retreat ignored those who had to remain behind: the poor and the sick in their slum environment.[18] So, if progress did occur it was beneficial to the few. The children who belonged to those few benefited from the ample play space incorporated into suburban design.[19]

However the coming of the park brought with it a measure of freedom for those left behind in the great metropolises; the design of which sparked a tendency to incorporate certain aspects of its design and planning into the general scheme of the city.[20] Lewis Mumford says that the city "...is a multi-form non-segregated environment,"[21] but this does not quite ring true either in the *Invisible Man* or in the history of Manchester. There "was" segregation. Edward I started it by passing a law making it illegal for Jews to live in England; a law not repealed until the 1650's. It is ironic that although Shakespeare invented the Shylock character in his play *The Merchant of Venice*, there were no Jews in London or Manchester at the time. Even when Jews did come to both cities in the nineteenth and twentieth centuries they remained - and still are - segregated although the segregation is really imposed from within their own communities: a kind of self-imposed exile.[22]

Another example of segregation in the city can be seen in Manchester. Economic progress came to the city in the form of trade - when the Chinese came to Liverpool from Canton -

of tea and silk.[23] But again, like the Jews, they have tended to segregate themselves from the rest of the community.

Modern signs of dystopia

The imprisonment of man through suburban progress is not limited to days gone by; it is a phenomenon which extends to the 21st century and takes the form of "segregation from reality." It is the suburban architect of democratic progress turned "Benefactor." Harmony is achieved but it is monotonous and devoid of freedom. Just as the mills of Manchester controlled the worker in the 19th century, Mumford details the control of contemporary suburban man through mass production:

> [There is a]...new kind of community...which caricature[s] both the historic city and the archetypal urban refuge: a multitude of uniform, unidentifiable houses, lined up inflexibly, at uniform distances, on uniform roads, in a treeless communal waste, inhabited by people of the same class, the same income, the same age group, witnessing the same television performances, eating the same tasteless pre-fabricated foods, from the same freezers, conforming in every outward and inward respect to a common mould, manufactured in the central metropolis.[24]

Mumford is saying here that progress does not engender freedom, but is destroyed by the necessities of function. The only real progress of the modern city is what he calls "...a better order of planning..."[25]

One of the few forms of freedom and autonomy modern man has inherited from his past is the freedom to drive the car on the suburban road system; but even this is mandatory if one wants to operate in society.[26] In short, the car does not offer progress or freedom as one would expect. Indeed it wastes time through congestion, and its related necessity the car park, devours much needed space.[27] The widespread use of the motor car is the antithesis of progress because function has become more important than harmony.[28]

The biggest insight of Ellison and Mumford is that dystopia is not the shadow of some city far off in the distant future, as in Zamytin's *We*, but is here with us now. This is evidenced no more clearly than when Mumford talks about the housewife who cannot make herself understood by the one-way communication of the television; or the person controlled by mass communication because those who operate the media own the right for us to communicate with each other. Mumford says of technological progress:

> Each member of suburbia becomes imprisoned by the very separation that he has prized: he is fed through a narrow opening: a telephone line, a radio band, a television circuit...[which]...is an organic by-product of an economy that sacrifices human development to mechanical processing.[29]

Mumford successfully conveys the impression that dystopia has already arrived and that "...the ultimate effect of the suburban escape in our time is, ironically, a low-grade uniform environment from which escape is impossible."[30] The "suburbian" inhabits nothing more than a monotonous functional suburbanscape, akin to Mumford's *Brief Outline of Hell*[31]

In order to escape our imprisonment, we must use what we have learnt from other great historical cities and take action to try and improve the freedom of the individual within the landscape he inherits; for as Mumford states, "...the city should be an organ of love."[32] Freedom calls us to action. Witness Ellison's most succinct conclusion, "Without the possibility of action, all knowledge comes to one labelled 'file and forget'..."[33] Maybe that is why I-330 is such a powerful figure in Zamyatin's futuristic story, because she directs all citizens of the metropolis to action, and urges us - just like she does D-503 - to be something more than we are. In battling the forces of authority, progress and the impulse of the individual, is she not Sophocle's heroine Antigone, projected onto the stage of postmodern eternity?

Notes

[1] Yevgeny Zamyatin, *We*, (New York: Penguin, 1993) introd. xv.

[2] B.F.Skinner, "Walden Two: Selections," *Philosophy and Contemporary Issues*, ed. John R. Burr, Milton Goldinger (New Jersey: Prentice-Hall, 1996) 55-68.

[3] Joseph Wood Krutch, "Ignoble Utopias," *Philosophy and Contemporary Issues*, ed. John R. Burr, Milton Goldinger (New Jersey: Prentice-Hall, 1996) 69-78.

[4] Ralph Ellison, *Invisible Man* (New York: Vintage International, 1980) 510.

[5] Ellison introd. xx.

[6] Ellison 243.

[7] Ellison 170.

[8] Zamyatin 45.

[9] Lewis Mumford, *The City in History: Its Origins, Its Transformations, and Its Prospects* (New York: Harcourt, Brace & World, Inc., 1961) 482.

[10] Mumford 484-85.

[11] Mumford 488.

[12] Bamber Gascoigne, *Encyclopedia of Britain* (Basingstoke: Macmillan, 1993) 402.

[13] Gascoigne 159.

[14] Zamyatin introd. xix.

[15] Gascoigne 487-88.

[16] Gascoigne 213, 402.

[17] Mumford 492.

[18] Mumford 494.

[19] Mumford 495.
[20] Mumford 489.
[21] Mumford 493.
[22] Gascoigne 337-38.
[23] Gascoigne 134.
[24] Mumford 486.
[25] Mumford 486.
[26] Mumford 492-93.
[27] Mumford 507.
[28] Mumford 508-509.
[29] Mumford 512-513.
[30] Mumford 486.
[31] Mumford 556.
[32] Mumford 575.
[33] Ellison 579.

Morris and Skinner on Social Control

Showing the structure and effects of governance and social control has been a common theme in utopian and dystopian fiction and follows a long literary tradition including George Orwell's *1984*, Aldous Huxley's *Brave New World* and Yevgeny Zamyatin's *We.*[1] In the case of William Morris's *News From Nowhere*, Utopia is projected forth from the 19th century into the future; and in B. F. Skinner's *Walden Two*, Utopia is set up in post-war, modern-day America using "behavioural engineering"[2] - a kind of scientific equivalent of the "table of hours" in Zamyatin's "OneState."[3] Interestingly, Joseph Wood Krutch points out that, "...whereas Plato's *The Republic* and Thomas More's *Utopia* are noble absurdities, [B. F. Skinner's] *Walden Two* is an ignoble one..."[4] Morris's Utopia definitely falls into the absurd category with the idea that man has progressed into the future without the evils of technology and with overtones of the Middle Ages.[5] As James Redmond says: "...it becomes plain that Morris is talking a good deal of nonsense."[6] Even Skinner's character Frazier agrees: "Many parts of *News From Nowhere* are ridiculous..."[7]

In *Walden Two*, the whole debate concerning the legitimacy of social control through "human conditioning" is presented in the form of a novel where the main characters, Castle and Frazier, represent the different sides of the moral argument.[8]

Both Skinner and Morris see a basic flaw in the human-societal system. For Skinner, social control is brought about by offsetting negative behavioural outcomes; by neutralizing the private, selfish desires of the individual from birth. As Frazier declares: "...when a particular emotion is no longer a useful part of a behavioural repertoire, we proceed to eliminate it. It's simply a matter of behavioural engineering."[9] Morris's solution on the other hand, is workable through the victory of socialism over capitalism and industrialism.[10]

Interestingly, when Redmond remarks that for Morris, Marxism "...offered...a modern revelation of the great pattern in human life"[11] one realizes that Frazier - who is like the faceless suburban architect known as the "Benefactor" in *We*[12] - has also found a great pattern, through an offshoot of reinforcement theory.[13]

What both Morris and Skinner share in their respective Utopias is a society without any form of political system. As Morris's Hammond says to "Guest": "I must now shock you by telling you that we have no longer anything which you, a native of another planet, would call a government."[14] Frazier also thinks that politics is a useless means of achieving Utopia, although he admits of the need for a "Board of Planners."[15]

Although the method of social control in Skinner's Walden Two community and Morris's "ancient-future paradise" mean crime free communities, the methods of achieving this state of affairs differ markedly.[16] For Skinner, behavioural engineering is the key behind controlling society; the episode with the sheep and the electric fence being an apt metaphor for the Walden Two establishment as a whole.[17] In contrast, Morris is in effect admitting that there is no formal methodology when he declares that, "...a tradition or habit of life has been growing on us; and that habit has become a habit of acting on the whole for the best. That is in short the foundation of our life and happiness."[18] Perhaps the controlling influence behind the lack of crime in Morris's world is simply due to the fact that just as "...in a society of equals you will not find any one to play the part of torturer or jailer..." perhaps also one cannot find anyone to assume the role of criminal.[19] And the Walden Two community evidently does not need laws to maintain social control, for the "...[Walden] code...keep[s] things running smoothly..."[20]

If Morris's society really is controlled by "habit" this means that the basis of this control originates in the past; there is no need for any kind of enforcing of behaviour because tradition maintains it.[21] Interestingly, in *Walden Two*, Frazier also admits that control originates in the past when he says that "...Walden Two is predetermined...Set it up right, and it will run by itself."[22] Despite the contrast in the way social control is brought about between Morris[23] and Skinner however, both Hammond and Frazier are influenced by the philosophy of Jesus Christ.[24]

In controlling the way their respective Utopian communities evolve, Both Skinner and Morris's decision-making policies are based on a system which reflects the mass or number of citizens. For example, in *News From Nowhere*, Hammond declares: "...when the matter is of common interest to the whole community...the majority must have their way...the apparent majority *is* the real majority..."[25] [author's italics]. Frazier also expresses the importance of the group.[26]

The Guest and Castle are both curious about how work behaviour is controlled. In *News From Nowhere* the Guest inquires, "...how [do] you get people to work when there is no reward of labour...?"[27] In Frazier's social experiment, people are content to work partly because they only have to do it four hours a day, and partly because Frazier uses the somewhat unconvincing excuse that "The really intelligent man doesn't want to feel that his work is being done by anyone else."[28] Of course, in *News From Nowhere*, the social system is based on a leisured class of citizens; the country does not impose any form of social control on the boat man, he works for free[29]; while in *Walden Two*, Frazier despises the leisured class as a "cancer", and yet clearly contradicts himself when he says that artists should be granted the freedom of leisure.[30]

Conclusion

In comparing and contrasting governance and social control in the Utopias exemplified in *Walden Two* and *News From Nowhere*, one can see that because scientific behavioural control techniques are not used to maintain social control in Morris's world, then the supervision of the community to which the Guest is introduced is perhaps the more natural way of determining the behaviour of citizens. Frazier uses "experimental" behavioural engineering to achieve social control right from the cradle.[31] It is an artificial "tolerance building" system offering less scope for personal choice.[32] But that is the whole point; the philosophy behind it echoes of Jeremy Bentham.[33] [34] [35] Frazier is more concerned with group rather than individual consciousness.[36] As Castle says to Frazier, "Then you don't offer complete personal freedom, do you?"[37] Even when Frazier insists that his society "...provide[s] a broad experience and many attractive alternatives" one is not readily convinced of this argument when he admits that his society is "predetermined."[38]

Both Morris's and Skinner's Utopia share the ideals that socialism originally sought - equality and the abolition of the class system. Frazier has even helped to ensure this by a society without honorific titles.[39]

Whereas according to Frazier, the notion of societal restraint in *Walden Two* "...exists right here and now!"[40] that in *News From Nowhere* is dreamlike, lacks the potency of reality and therefore is nothing more than a romantic vision.[41] But if this is true, is the system of the Walden Two community any better? Perhaps the last word should rest with Steve, who momentarily questions the validity of it all: "Things like that aren't free. There must be some catch."[42]

Notes

[1] Clarence Brown, *We,* trans. By Yevgeny Zamyatin. (New York: Penguin, 1993) introd. xv.
[2] B. F., Skinner, *Walden Two* (New Jersey: Prentice-Hall, 1976) 10.
[3] Brown introd. xix.
[4] Joseph Wood Krutch, "Ignoble Utopias." *Philosophy and Contemporary Issues.* Ed. John R. Burr, Milton Goldinger. (New Jersey: Prentice-Hall, 1996) 69-78
[5] James Redmond, ed. Introduction. *News From Nowhere.* By William Morris. 1891. (London: Routledge, 1992). intro. xxx-xxxi.
[6] Redmond intro. xxiv.
[7] Skinner 165.
[8] John R. Burr, John R., and Milton Goldinger., ed. *Philosophy and Contemporary Issues.* 7th ed. (New Jersey: Prentice-Hall, 1996) 31-2.
[9] Skinner 89, 93.
[10] William Morris, *News From Nowhere.* 1891. Ed. James Redmond. (London: Routledge, 1992) xxv, xxvi, xxxvii.
[11] Redmond xxv.
[12] Yevgeny Zamyatin, *We.* Trans. Clarence Brown. (New York: Penguin, 1993) 46.
[13] Skinner 244.
[14] Morris 63.
[15] Skinner 10, 48, 180.
[16] Morris xxxiii.
[17] Skinner 10, 15.
[18] Morris 67.
[19] Morris 71.
[20] Skinner 95, 150.
[21] Morris 67, 78.
[22] Skinner 219, 238-9.
[23] Morris 70.
[24] Skinner 245.
[25] Morris 74.

[26] Skinner 95, 149-50.
[27] Morris 77.
[28] Skinner 50, 52.
[29] Morris 7-8.
[30] Skinner 50, 80.
[31] Skinner 89, 101.
[32] Skinner 97.
[33] Bamber Gascoigne, *Encyclopedia of Britain.* (Basingstoke: Macmillan, 1993) 60.
[34] Margaret Nicholas, *The World's Greatest Cranks and Crackpots.* 2nd ed. (London: Hamlyn, 1997) 84-6.
[35] Skinner 162.
[36] Skinner 89, 95, 182.
[37] Skinner 47.
[38] Skinner 239.
[39] Skinner 49.
[40] Skinner 179.
[41] Morris xxxvii.
[42] Skinner 168.

CHAPTER 2

Dystopia Now: Some Contemporary Issues

Freedom and Pornography: Who Does Freedom Belong to?

Pornography is a topic which is one of the feminists' strongest resources in attempts to gain an increasing membership of their exclusive club. Males along with non-feminists are of course excluded. The topic has a popular following along the feminist movement because members are faced with a problem for *them,* of a sandwich of entertainment and art in a particular seductive form.

Pornography has always generated a limited form of offence; limited because the negative feelings it generates are, on the whole, restricted to women who are not consumers of such merchandise which is available in adult shops and bookstores. They are not consumers because it is usually their own sex represented on the covers, between the pages of the magazines and in the fictional teleplays represented on DVD. *Fictional* is of course the key word to be taken note of here. The definition in my dictionary gives "fiction" as "The act or art of feigning or inventing."[1] Stating the definition is important because it reminds us that what is fictionalized or invented is different from reality or from the real world; as night is different from day.

Let us look at some of the tentative arguments put forward by feminists like Helen E. Longino who is appealing for the prohibition of pornography.[2] Longino wants pornography banned because, in her estimation, it is part of sexism and sexual inequality, and as they are both wrong, so must pornography be wrong. I dissent from Longino, however, regarding the idea that pornography is sexist and sexually unequal. I assert they are not because for something to be sexist and unequal, it must a) be real, b) propagate a specific message whose aim can be proven to attempt to change the behaviour and attitude of its audience, in this case men, and c) offer evidence that it represents the actual views of its creator/artist. Neither a), b) nor c) are true and neither can their veracity be proven. First of all, pornography is not real because it is invented. Once the photography session or filming is finished, the actors and actresses - and let us acknowledge they are nothing else but the work they do - reassume their normal identities, receive payment for their work and return home. Secondly, there is no concrete message directed to the male audience to effect behavioural or attitudinal change. Any manifestation of behaviour or attitude is already latent in the audience; the pornographic stimulus simply triggers and encourages it to manifest itself in the form of sexual excitement which is a pleasurable emotion. Also, how could anyone seriously assert that any real message is being propagated in an art medium devoid of any dialogue? Finally, in art and entertainment, it is not a matter for us to question the possible views of the director, cameraman or artist except in the context of satisfying a superficial artistic curiosity. Indeed, aside from interviewing the director, how can we determine if the material is an accurate reflection of the views of the creator?

The next argument that Longino puts forward for the abolition of pornography is tied up with her redefinition of it. Pornography is not the sexually explicit material itself: the photographs, magazines and films, for these are only two-dimensional images; it is the act of endorsing such things that constitutes pornography. The act of endorsing it, is, apparently, the reason to abolish it. The point requires little in the way of answering because I have already made it quite clear that to prove endorsing actually occurs, we would have to know the real intent of the creator of the pornographic product, and only lawyers, journalists and psychiatrists are in the business of dealing with, and investigating, people's motives. In addition, to paraphrase Jan Narveson, do artists and creators actually and consistently represent their true beliefs in artistic form?[3] And even if they perchance do, how do we prove it? If we really believed it, would not those in power ban all war films because their directors believe soldiers and innocent civilians deserve to die in wartime. I therefore cannot accept Longino's argument that the creators of pornography actually endorse it. Neither can I accept her assertion that pornography endorses and increases female social, economic and cultural oppression.

Longino seems to be perpetuating unsubstantiated accusations of sexism and inequality, instead of recognising the pornographic product for what it really is: an aspect of artistic free expression, whose purpose is only to sexually arouse the audience in an entertaining manner.

Longino believes that pornography perpetuates the sexual inequality of men and women, although I suspect she is only thinking of women. I believe that such sexual inequality has always existed, and always will; not because of pornography, but because of physical and mental - in terms of male and female perception of sexual experience - differences. And I use the term "inequality" in the sense of difference, not injustice. What is physical and mental is, biologically speaking, obviously not manmade and therefore cannot be unjust. There are countless books currently on the market, which attest to the mental and emotional differences between men and women. Some conclude quite openly that man does not equal woman either emotionally or perceptually, which is something most of mankind has suspected for thousands of years. It has been shown time and time again that men and women want different things from their sexual experience, and to assert wrongly, as feminists do, that men and women should be the same is to forcibly ignore their differences; differences which constitute identity.

Pornography has always been objectionable, and not only to feminists. Originally it was found objectionable on semi-religious grounds. Any way of thinking which put forward a view of sex as something to be enjoyed apart from the act of procreation was seen as anathema to the religious community. Then it was a matter taken up by those who saw the bounds of common decency being invaded by, at first, underground currents proposing a permissiveness which turned into the sexual revolution of the 1960s and 1970s. Now it is the turn of the feminists to continue the debate and push for prohibition; but prohibition will never come about because you cannot impose feminist ways of thinking on people, for example, on a male audience, just because their standards of decency and aesthetics differ from the feminist criteria of equality.

Longino asserts that a) "women are represented as passive" and b) "...women's sexual pleasure is ...subordinate to that of men and is never an end in itself as is the sexual pleasure of men." If one looks at the wide-ranging selection of pornographic DVD material available on the market, one will see that this statement is in fact untrue. Some *male* characters, for instance, desire to be controlled by the woman in the sex-play. This suggests to me that the raw material on which Longino bases her opinion is abnormally selective.

I dispute also, Longino's belief in the fact that actors and actresses who consent to be abused in pornography does nothing to ameliorate the degrading nature of it. I assert that they are not being abused but are acting or pretending within a work environment. Again, let us remind ourselves that pornography is *fictional*, something which Longino chooses to avoid discussing. Nobody says that actors and actresses in the cinema degrade themselves by pretending to kill each other, pretending to make love, pretending to cry, pretending to feel happy or sad, or indeed pretending to do any other mode of human behaviour, because the audience see the actors and actresses - as they do themselves - as part of a noble profession. Some critics might of course contend that a movie based on one of Shakespeare's plays is nobler than a movie about sex; but that of course is a matter of personal taste and opinion; and notions of proper taste are not the exclusive right of the feminist. Longino is rendering her private dislikes in a public theatre.

She further criticises the fantasies of the pornographic audience, as if it were some negative state of mind; but what person does not partially "enter" the role of a character or characters in a play, film or book? Is that not also fantasy? Is the feminist not mocking our right to escape from our everyday lives? Fantasy is a very important part of our lives. And when Longino declares, "...pornography must lie," surely she means "pretend" because again let us remind ourselves that we are dealing with fictional entertainment not reality. Perhaps pornography is indeed pretending; so what else is new in the entertainment world?

The notion that pornography creates the impression of women being accessible to rape, torture and murder is a gross exaggeration and erroneous at one and the same time. Feminists constantly protest at the degree of violence in sex films. However, there are two points to note: a) There are numerous books, magazines and DVDs which contain violence, as well as films showing at the cinema, and nobody is reacting in the way the feminists are; and b) violence, like sex in movies and DVDs is, at the sake of repeating myself again, only play-acting. Feminists want greater censorship so that such materials are not made accessible to the public. However, if the government were to completely prohibit sexual materials also containing violence, liberal principles would be at risk and members of the public would be denied the right of personal choice. In my estimation, consumers of pornographic products would object to the conservative approach of government deciding what is good or bad for them. People want to have the right to decide for themselves about the kind of products they want to buy, without government interference.

Another reason why feminists are against the producing and selling of so-called violent sex films is because they declare that there is a causal relation between such materials and illegal sexual and violent acts of behaviour against women; but, as Jan Narveson points out, the evidence for this is extremely weak to say the least. Further, despite Longino's assertion, pornography in no way condones crimes against women, nor is there any connection between pornography and the social, economic and cultural oppression of women. If Longino is adamant that this is not the case, the responsibility to explain further the pertinent reasons why this is so, lies with her. This is something she has so far failed to do to my satisfaction. In addition, she asserts that pornography isolates women from the political arena because it reinforces the belief that women are sexually unequal. The fact that women are sexually unequal - or perhaps sexually "dissimilar" is a better word - is something I concede. Indeed, I have pointed out precisely why this divergence of sexuality exists, earlier in these writings. Even by a huge stretch of the imagination, however, I fail to see how the biological and perceptual sexual differences of women can determine their political status.

Longino also harps on about the explicit nature of pornographic magazine covers in bookshops and grocery stores. However, if one looks at the other selection of magazines on sale, it is evident that they too give examples of the magazine's content on the cover. It is simply advertising, and is of course necessary so that the consumer's attention is attracted to it and will buy it. The same goes for magazines about cars, fishing or computer products. Why does Longino not become angry at the sight of a gleaming sports car on the cover of a car magazine or a naked fish on the cover of a fishing magazine?

I maintain that no harm is done to the purchasers of pornographic materials; and none is done to the public either, except in the form of offence, which is simply a reaction to personal taste. To object to pornography simply on grounds of individual taste is to suggest the legitimacy of imposing one's standards onto others. For the feminist movement, of course, such an imposition has engendered an almost cult following on behalf of its followers. However, a cult may be defined as a puny group whose supporters would not signify even marginal consequence.

Solid evidence of the harmful effects of pornography is still not forthcoming. The display of emotion and rhetoric by feminists is a reflection of their private aesthetic concerns. The feminist should consider the following above all else: one woman in a pornographic photograph or DVD, is in no way intended to, and indeed cannot, represent the whole of womankind. Neither can the actress cause other women to behave in the same way. Indeed, how can women be influenced at all by such visual representation when they do not constitute the marginal viewing audience?

In my view, as long as pornography is kept within the adult world, then like free speech, people should be left to make up their own minds. Child pornography is of course a different matter. Children are not old enough to make decisions that may affect them later in life. Directors and photographers who exploit them are criminals and should be prosecuted with the full force of the law.

In conclusion, Longino's view is feminist centred. She is asserting that all adults who consent to have sex do so in terms of *her* own ideals and sexual preferences. This anti-relativist stance does not take into account the willingness of actors and actresses, many of whom enjoy working in the world of pornography. Those who take part do so because they desire to; and because they receive high payment for their efforts. One cannot talk about the abuse of human dignity when people choose to have these experiences. In addition, people purchase and enjoy these products because they want to. Who could possibly have the temerity to deny them otherwise?

Notes

[1] Arthur L. Hayward and John J. Sparkes, *The Concise English Dictionary*, 4th ed., (London: New Orchard) 1992.
[2] Helen E. Longino, "Pornography, Oppression, and Freedom: A closer Look," *Philosophy and Contemporary Issues*, 7th ed., (New Jersey: Prentice Hall) 1996, 326-37.
[3] Jan Narveson, "Pornography," *Philosophy and Contemporary Issues*, 7th ed., (New Jersey: Prentice Hall) 1996, 338-50.

Same-Sex Marriage

Should gay and lesbian couples be allowed to marry? That is the question which is still the focus of political and moral debate for the homosexual and religious community.[1] In America, it was the state of Hawaii which started the controversy when it was thought that same-sex marriages were to be legally sanctioned. However, this was quelled by the United States Congress passing "The Defense of Marriage Act" (DOMA) in 1996.[2] In essence, the act only recognizes a marriage between a man and a woman. Towards the end of the 1990's, similar bills were approved by various states.

Proponents of same-sex unions point out that not only will couples benefit, but the community as well. They believe that married couples will be psychologically and physically healthier. If they marry, long-term relationships will become the norm; this in turn will reduce promiscuity and lessen the spread of aids and other sexually transmitted diseases, which in turn would reduce the cost of health care.

Is marriage purely a written contract? Gay and lesbian couples would answer "No" because one of the things they feel is unfair, is that if they are denied marriage, they are automatically denied monetary, social and psychological benefits also. Homosexuals contend that this government denial of, what they see as the basic rights of citizens, amounts to discrimination; but those against such marriages contend that sanctioning them would destroy the traditional institution of marriage. John Finnis for example, maintains that homosexual marriage is wrong because it would only satisfy the personal needs of the couple, who are unable to unite biologically and therefore cannot serve society by producing offspring and continuing the human race.[3] Other critics declare that same-sex unions would threaten traditional notions of the family which is, in their view, an essential component of a healthy society.

Homosexuals are obviously dissatisfied with the institution of marriage as it stands now. However, they are not alone in their viewpoint. Feminists too, are unhappy with marriage, but for different reasons. Homosexual couples are unhappy because they are excluded from marriage; feminists are unhappy because they believe marriage is oppressive. Feminists are not so much trying to modify marriage, as bring down its foundations and start from scratch. Despite the apparent similarity of purpose, feminists are only interested in seeking their own goals: that of depowering the traditional patriarchal society and creating more opportunities for themselves. Cheshire Calhoun believes lesbian-feminists have the capacity to destroy the traditional image of the subordinate wife in the family, and reject the notion that women exist only to perform the maternal and domestic imperative.[4]

Lesbian-feminists use the term nonparticipation to summarize their rejection of all forms of marriage and family life. Personally, I fail to see why lesbian-feminists oppose the state of marriage at all, for although they criticize the traditional male-centred marriage, in their own marriages they would surely redefine the traditional family roles into terms of their own liking.

One government policy that would ameliorate the dissatisfaction of gay couples would be the introduction of a new benefits system, which all members of the community would be entitled to. The demand by same-sex couples for these benefits raises an important question: do they really want an officially recognized marriage, or simply the financial benefits that accompany it? Ruth Colker maintains that one of the problems with marriage as it now stands, is that the marriage-dependent benefits system fosters the notion that marriage is a one-way ticket to government benefits, and thus financial security.[5] Whatever arguments the government puts forward as a way of excuse, denying homosexuals marriage is denying them a right to which other members of the community are entitled.

John Finnis, drawing on Plato, Aristotle, Plutarch, Kant and others, chastises homosexual conduct on the grounds that it, along with masturbation and other forms of non-marital sex, is an expression of purely selfish behaviour. For Finnis, sexual behaviour is inextricably linked to the more useful act of procreation, for it is behaviour which is intended to serve mankind, not personal gratification. Indeed he labels those who commit any form of sexual activity outside of marriage illusion seekers. The two main points in Finnis' argument which engender a dichotomy in our (his and mine) thinking are firstly, a) His definition of "good," and b) his linking of gaming and sexual activities. Let us take a) first. Finnis uses the term "good" in two ways. He first of all uses it when he talks about procreation being the common good, in that it serves the purpose for which mankind was intended: the continuation of the human race. Secondly, Finnis uses "good" as some sort of philosophical bi-product of human activity. For Finnis, other activities like sports, for instance, give pleasure and are good. Illicit sexual behaviour on the other hand, although giving pleasure, is not good. In looking at b), Finnis accuses those who commit illicit sex of viewing it as a mere game. He then talks about why sexual activity differs from games. Is he really assuming that people genuinely view sex in this way? Who says they do? And who says that only games, eating, dancing and non-sexually related activities are good? I beg to differ; Finnis is simply expressing his definition of good as he sees fit. And nobody said sex was a game, save Finnis himself.

Some feminists however, are also against same-sex marriage. Nan Hunter believes that if the government permitted it, marriage and notions of the family as they are now would be destabilized.[6] Mary Dunlap says marriage can be constructive and wants to see the debate break out of the legal stranglehold which currently encompasses it.[7] Barbara J. Cox suggests that in the case of feminists who are also lesbians, there is an ambiguity and dilemma in the prospect of marriage.[8] They want the right to marry like heterosexual couples, but also acknowledge that marriage introduces women to domestic slavery. Cox, however, ends on a positive note when she disclaims that feminist-lesbians compromise their principles by marrying. She draws on her own positive experiences of a lesbian wedding which she maintains was not a tacit acceptance of patriarchal society and convention, but an affirmation of her identity and power as an individual; an individual who just so happens to prefer the same sex.

Some of the most accessible reasons for the government recognizing same-sex marriages is given by Adrian Alex Wellington, when he declares that having the right to be able to choose a same-sex marriage is warranted in any society which holds freedom and liberalism as its most cherished values.[9] He is saying that the government no longer has the right - if it ever had it in the first place - to dictate to people their definition of good and bad, normal and abnormal. In other words, all people should be free to choose the lifestyle they wish to pursue. Wellington further maintains that what happens in the bedroom of a couple, whether heterosexual or homosexual, is of no concern whatever to the state, unless harm occurs to its citizens. Wellington also points out that heterosexual and homosexual relationships are, on a functional level, equal. Indeed, he emphasizes the importance of the functional aspect of marriage above all else, and only seeks government legislative reform to actualize the wishes of the homosexual community for whom he speaks. According to Wellington's tenet, in order to maintain social justice in a liberal and free society, the state is obligated to sanction homosexual relationships through the endorsement of same-sex marriage. In other words, Wellington's political philosophy dictates that for true liberalism to be realized, support of homosexual unions is a key factor. For Wellington, ignoring the desires of the homosexual community and not permitting them to marry if they so wish, is to define state notions of what normality and correctness are, and impose them on people without any regard for the right of the individual's emotional nature and the freedom of choice.

Wellington also raises some interesting points regarding the inadequacy of the state image of matrimonial propriety. Many couples do have extra-marital affairs, and many couples marry for companionship, not the production of children. Even homosexuals and heterosexuals sometimes marry each other despite the incompatibility of their sexual preferences. Therefore, what is required is a concept of marriage which allows for the fluidity of personal desire and individual context. In other words, a service should be offered by the state, which is essentially the official sanctioning of a union of two people whoever they may be, and whatever sexual inclinations they may have. Wellington goes on to say that marriage as it realistically functions today, is independent of sexual and emotional practices. The only justification that the government can give for prohibiting same-sex marriages would fall into the category of discrimination.

Some of those against same-sex marriages reject it because of the religious foundations of matrimony. James Q. Wilson, quotes Leviticus who declares that, "...[man] liv[ing] with mankind as with womankind...is an abomination..."[10] Thus, if homosexual marriages are validated, the sacred traditional marriage will be harmed; but not harm in the sense one might conceive it; rather the meaning of marriage would be modified. To give a rather exaggerated example, one of the gay partners wearing a wedding dress at the ceremony would be a grotesque imitation of the real thing. Some sort of adequate apparel would be necessary. There would of course have to be linguistic modifications too: terms like "husband" and "wife," and "bride" and "groom" would perhaps become obsolete.

There are those, however, who would say that marriage would harm the struggle of the gay rights and feminist movements. The feminists deplore the patriarchy of marriage; the homosexuals demand the equality of it. Homosexuals gaining access to the institution of marriage would endorse the importance of male domination; and the feminists succeeding in rejecting legislation for same-sex unions would detract from the equality the gay community is seeking.

Andrew Sullivan, himself a homosexual, in discussing the accusation that same-sex marriages would threaten traditional heterosexual marriages, believes that if the government fails to endorse same-sex unions, they are effectively perpetuating an homophobic reaction to the homosexual community.[11] Even the homosexual's mother, father and other family members would be influenced by the climate of public disapproval, eventually rejecting their homosexual sons, daughters, brothers and sisters, and leading ultimately to the wrecking of family life. Sullivan says same-sex marriages need to be introduced in order to encourage long-term relationships and all the security for the individual and the community that entails. However, James Q. Wilson referring to Sullivan's book *Virtually Normal* talks of the pessimistic attitude of Sullivan with respect to the permanence of gay marriage and the homosexual couple's obligation to it.

The lesbian-feminist Cheshire Calhoun presents a very different perspective on the virtue of long-term, monogamous relationships when she speaks of the homosexual community's "...assumption that [such] relationships are more valuable than any other kind of relationship."[12] Perhaps Calhoun believes that promiscuity is the ideal way of life for single-parent families, lesbians and feminists. She goes on to say of gay and straight women:

"[Their]...interests [lie] in objecting to a social and legal system that privileges long-term, monogamous relationships over all other forms of relationship."[13]

Calhoun's viewpoint is radical and far from discriminating. She uses some clever neologisms to reinforce her rhetoric: terms such as "familial outlaws," "nonparticipation" and "feminization of poverty." "Familial outlaws" refers to the social constructionist view of lesbians as something alienated from marriage, family and mothering. "Nonparticipation" is one of those neutral, unemotional words, which cleverly disguises this state of self-inflicted lesbian-feminist alienation; and "feminization of property" conjures up the misguided notion that all divorced women with children are financially disadvantaged. Calhoun continues that lesbian-feminists should, "...assert their deviance from the category *woman*."[14] I agree, facetiously of course, that lesbians are deviants; not because of their sexuality, but because of their preference - if we are to accept Calhoun's notions of normal unions - for short-term and unstable relationships.

At the moment there are no incentives for gay and lesbians to behave in responsible and virtuous ways. I think this is simply because homosexuals are identified by their public behaviour and by their private sexual acts; the state, with support from the Church, automatically classifying the people who commit sodomy un-virtuous and incapable of redemption.

Andrew Sullivan further points out that as an homosexual marriage would be imitating a stable heterosexual one, and as a heterosexual union is the state ideal, heterosexual marriage would thereby be indirectly endorsed and its importance socially and psychologically would be highlighted and strengthened.

Sullivan argues that the homosexual community's demand for equality in marriage is rooted in conservatism. This is because homosexuals only want access to a basic human right, and because they do not seek to destabilize the Church by changing marriage. Indeed, Sullivan maintains that the seeking of marriage licences is a purely civil matter, and is separate from the Church - an institution Sullivan concedes is deliberating fairly over the same-sex marriage issue. Personally, I agree that gays and lesbians are fighting a conservative cause; they must be, as they are only seeking an official endorsement of fidelity, monogamy and the chance to commit themselves to the stability of family life.

William Bennett says that homosexuals want to be permitted to marry; being excluded from this civil and religious convention is tantamount to officially sanctioned discrimination, discrimination which is based on their preference for unconventional sexual partners.[15] That much is true. However, if we allow gays and lesbians access to the marriage ceremony, why can we not allow father and daughter to marry, or two sisters or two brothers to marry each other; or brother and sister to marry each other for that matter? Bennet's point that Sullivan is basing his notion of equality solely on a relativist criteria, and has therefore deserted his moral perspicacity, is a valid one.

I think Sullivan's point about the American congress asking why polygamy should not also be permitted if same-sex marriages are, is worthy of note. I also agree with Sullivan when he says that, "...polygamy is an *activity*, whereas both homosexuality and heterosexuality are *states*."[16] But I think this really is a side issue unrelated to the real discussion of whether to allow same-sex marriage. After all, who would want to see mother and son, or brother and sister marry? But according to Sullivan's definition of equality and fair play, such things should be permitted.

Nevertheless, Bennett's point about why fathers and daughters, brothers and sisters and the like should not be eligible to marry does not take into account an important consideration: a father who is prevented by law from marrying his daughter does have a choice: he can find another partner who is of similar age, and more importantly, is not a family member. However, a gay man who has - to use Sullivan's quote - an "objective disorder," does not have the same choice because he is biologically, and therefore naturally disposed to, coupling with a person of the same sex. So even if he were to decline the attentions of one same-sex partner, he must choose the attentions of another because his sexual inclination dictates it.

In summary, those against same-sex unions argue that they threaten the healthy institution of marriage, endorse relationships which do not produce children and are therefore not beneficial to the community as a whole. But if they want to reduce the pressure from the gay rights movement in America, they should charge congress with reforming the benefits system so that government monies paid to the receivers are not tied to the state of marriage, but are independent of it.

If gay and lesbians are not allowed to marry, it will be interpreted as the government not endorsing long-term relationships; rather short-term ones, with all the promiscuity that entails. And if homosexuals were given the right to marry, would they all want to? And would not those who choose to reject marriage be marginalized by those who accepted it?

At any rate, if a marriage-dependent benefits system is maintained and gay and lesbians are excluded from marriage, the gay community will always have good reason to accuse the government of discriminating against minorities. However, I concede James Q. Wilson's point that society's rejection of homosexual marriage stems not from prejudice, but from opinion based on education; education demanded by the necessity of maintaining a family based society whose purpose is cohesion and procreation.

If one agrees with the postulations of figures like Adrian Alex Wellington, to embrace the virtue of homosexual marriage is to embrace liberalism. The philosophy of liberalism is the philosophy of equal rights for everybody. One cannot be a liberal and reject those goals the homosexual community seeks. To do so would be to create an illegitimate paradox whose resolution would only entail either unilaterally accepting both liberalism and the validity of full homosexual rights, or, rejecting both. Neither one nor the other can exist in isolation. Both demand a response from the individual and society in order for the principles of social justice to be held.

Interestingly, a positive response towards gay and lesbian marriage has been forthcoming, but from an unsuspected source, and for reasons not related to engendering equal opportunities, but financial ones. Shops and services in the wedding trade are flaunting the goods and services on offer to the gay community. Gay weddings are big business. Would it not be ironic if the bridal trade was the institution to turn the public's negative attitude towards gay weddings into the enthusiastic acceptance of a new social phenomenon?

Those who argue against same-sex unions cannot claim that any harm would come to society as a result of official sanctioning. Indeed the onus is on the state to prove that anything more than offence at the homosexual's freedom of choice is at work. It is a freedom of choice that requires a re-conception of marriage to make it valid.

The homosexual community is viewed by the rest of society and the government as apart from society because of their sexual preferences. Since the gay community is seeking to gain access to an institution to which the straight population has access, then to reject their wishes is to reject their attempts to assimilate into normal society and be recognized as normal human beings. They do not want anything extra, nor do they demand any special treatment; they are simply expressing their right to equality. Cheshire

Calhoun and Judith Stacey,[17] along with Frank Browning,[18] in defining more than one type of equality, is advocating a multiplicity of family patterns including polygamous, short-term ones, with the result that the term "family pattern" seems somewhat out of place. Perhaps "societal misfit syndrome" would be more appropriate to describe the reality of it all. Calhoun prefers Stacey's nicer sounding "postmodern family."

Notes

[1] Julie McDonald, "Same-Sex Marriage," *Contemporary Issues in a Diverse Society*, (Belmont: Wadsworth, 1998) 420-23.
[2] United States Congress, "The 1996 'Defense of Marriage Act,'" McDonald 446.
[3] John Finnis, "Homosexual Conduct is Wrong," McDonald 423-425.
[4] Cheshire Calhoun, "Family's Outlaws: Rethinking the Connections Between Feminism, Lesbianism, and the Family," McDonald 462-476.
[5] Ruth Colker, "Marriage," qtd. in Barbara J. Cox, "A Personal Essay on Same-Sex Marriage," McDonald 425-428.
[6] Nan D. Hunter, "Marriage Law and Gender," qtd. in Barbara J. Cox, "A Personal Essay on Same-Sex Marriage," McDonald 426.
[7] Mary Dunlap, "Symposium, The Family in the 1990s: An Exploration of Lesbian and Gay Rights." qtd. in Barbara J. Cox, "A Personal Essay on Same-Sex Marriage," McDonald 426.
[8] Barbara J. Cox, "A Personal Essay on Same-Sex Marriage," McDonald 425-428.
[9] Adrian Alex Wellington, "Why Liberals Should Support Same Sex Marriage," McDonald 428-446.

[10] James Q. Wilson, "Against Homosexual Marriage," McDonald 454-461.
[11] Andrew Sullivan, "The Conservative Case," McDonald 446-454.
[12] Cheshire Calhoun, "Family's Outlaws: Rethinking the Connections Between Feminism, Lesbianism, and the Family, McDonald 465.
[13] Cheshire Calhoun, "Family's Outlaws: Rethinking the Connections Between Feminism, Lesbianism, and the Family," McDonald 466.
[14] Cheshire Calhoun, "Family's Outlaws: Rethinking the Connections Between Feminism, Lesbianism, and the Family," McDonald 466.
[15] William Bennett, "Leave Marriage Alone," McDonald 451-452.
[16] Andrew Sullivan, "A Rely to Bennett," McDonald 452.
[17] Judith Stacey, qtd. in Calhoun, "Family's Outlaws: Rethinking the Connections Between Feminism, Lesbianism, and the Family," McDonald 471.
[18] Frank Browning "Why Marry?" McDonald 476-477.

The Death Penalty

As an English person, I regard the use of the death penalty system in the United States of America rather like a dilettante antiquarian regards an item of bric-a-brac in a junk shop. I notice an old typewriter in a corner of the shop and imagine some unimportant office girl just after the war, hammering on the keys, and banging out a memorandum for the faceless receiver. And I think about what a useful little instrument it was in its day. It isn't that it was a perfect mechanical wonder, because it wasn't; after all, one still had to learn to type in order to be able to use it effectively. One still had to hammer on the correct keys in the correct sequence otherwise a mistake would surely be apparent, all in black ink, upon the virgin white background. And one still had to fiddle about with the typewriter ribbon to get a decent printing of the font. However, it was the best implement around at the time. In spite of this, who would ever dream of using such an antique today? Today everything is hardware, software, hard-drives and CD ROMs. In the same way, are not the noose, guillotine, electric chair and poison-filled syringe, remnants of an outmoded judicial system? Yes, such things are relics of the past. Surely these antiques belong with other curiosities in museums for those patrons who have a morbid interest in primitive modes of cruelty as used in *ancient* times?

In England, executions were a form of punishment which had class distinctions. Those belonging to the aristocracy were beheaded, the rest of the criminal population being subjected to hanging, even for lesser crimes than murder. Up until the 18th century, executions took place in public, notably at Tyburn, where the residents of London were offered popular entertainment in the form of hangings.[1]

Having thus classified all the devices of capital punishment as savage antiques of bygone days, we look now at the current debate in America regarding the execution of criminals. In the U.S., it is the individual state which gives itself the authority to catch criminals, find them innocent or guilty, and sentence them to death. The legal system is part of the state and is free from criticism relating to the lawlessness of its punishment of the lawless.

Those for the death penalty argue that its use is a practical deterrent. Of course, if this were true, after the first few criminals were hanged, the state's aim would have been achieved, and no more murderers would have partaken of crime. As this merry hope has failed to materialize, the deterrent argument falls flat on its pathetic little face. Indeed, Ernest van den Haag, a proponent of the death penalty, is also unconvinced of the effectiveness of the death penalty as a deterrent when he admits, "Deterrence is not altogether decisive for me either."[2] Other proponents declare that murderers who are executed by the state deserve the punishment they receive.

Those against the death penalty usually raise the question of the savagery of the thing. They also point out that as the judicial process is less than perfect, innocents are bound to receive unjust deserts. And what can be more unjust and irreversible than death by execution? Even Ernest van den Haag acknowledges, "Because of the finality of the death penalty, the most grievous maldistribution occurs when it is imposed upon the innocent." I well remember reading accounts of such an incident occurring in 1949 when Timothy Evans, a mentally retarded tenant was hanged for the murder of his wife and baby whose bodies had been found in a shed in the garden of the house they were living in. It was later discovered, after the bodies of numerous other victims were found in the house, that the culprit was Evans's landlord, John Reginald Christie, who later confessed to all the murders of the victims, including Evans's wife. This case was an infamous one of injustice, and it played a leading role in the abolition of capital punishment in Britain in 1965.[3]

Social theorists argue that we should look closely at cases where defendants have been convicted and sentenced to death in order to see which members of society - their race and class - receive the death penalty. Critics point out that as society is unequal, with racism still apparent and a bias in favour of the wealthier sections of society, the state is unequal to the task of administering the death penalty fairly. Poorer sections of society, as is clearly apparent, are unable to pay the expenses of skilled lawyers. And those waiting on death row for the commencement of the state's final mockery of the sanctity of human life seem to consist of abnormal numbers of racial minorities. Proponents of the death penalty therefore have a humanitarian obligation to explain this discrepancy.

So far we have seen that doubts regarding the equity of death sentencing in the judicial system continue to raise their ugly heads, but is there any support from social science research that suggests the legal system is not fair? To answer that question, we will look at the results of the Baldus study.[4] The research team, lead by David Baldus of the University of Iowa, concluded that the death penalty was being administered unfairly in Georgia. Both victim and defendant racial factors were in evidence; indubitably so. In cases where the victim was white and the defendant black, the defendant was more likely to receive the death penalty than if the victim was black and the defendant white. Erik Eckholm says, "...the true bias arises from the race of the victim, regardless of the killer's race."[5] The disturbing figures are there in the study and cannot be disputed. What this means is that if you are a white defendant, you have a chance of avoiding execution, but if you are black, you are more likely to die at the hands of the state. Being black or white however, ought to be an irrelevant consideration in deciding innocence or guilt, and as

Professor Stephen Nathanson at Northeastern University says, "This is an important point. It certainly makes matters worse to decide deliberately to base life and death choices on irrelevant considerations."[6]

Both Nathanson and van den Haag respond perspicaciously to each other's opinions. The only point in van den Haag's rhetoric which I concede is worthy of note here however, is in his discussion of the arbitrary selection of certain individuals for execution among the guilty, which he feels is just; while the fact that those who escape justice by a fluke is unjust, because they are guilty too and also deserve punishment. Nathanson also points out that it is unfair to those who are punished if the rest of the guilty escape punishment. Both the arguments of van den Haag and Nathanson seem perfectly logical and they therefore appear justified in their respective viewpoints. However, as the death penalty is so final, and - to use van den Haag's example - receiving a speeding ticket is not, I would have to side with Nathanson. If you have a choice between a legal procedure which punishes a few people based on unfair criteria, and not having any procedure at all, but which permits fairness, it is better to have the latter. But van den Haag's answer to the problem of racism in the legal system is disturbingly clear when he says that discrimination against blacks in death sentencing should be remedied by executing more white people. Such an attitude is reckless and only serves to fan the flames of the death penalty debate. Van den Haag's philosophy does not solve the problem of racism at its roots, and therefore is at best a 'paper over the cracks' philosophy, and at worst an unpalatable obscenity.

The most incredible thing about the racism problem however, is that in spite of acknowledging the sovereign part racial factors play in death sentencing, the Supreme Court denied that the results of the Baldus study should influence the outcome of court sentencing. In a nutshell, this means that despite racism in the judicial system, death sentencing remains unchallenged. But how can this be when racism is itself a crime? The Supreme Court offers no satisfactory answer when it affirms the right of judges, prosecutors and jurors to be safe from any form of inquiry with regard to their decision making.

And so black people continue to be treated at a disadvantage and suffer from it. Perhaps, as van den Haag says, the defendant, who has committed an atrocious murder, does perceive a life sentence far worse than execution; but there is no way to determine whether this is the case or not. At any rate, to execute more black people than white people for the same crime, irrespective of their individual perceptions of life sentences and institutional death, is to signify that black people are more deserving of death than white people. Where is the logic and sanity in that?

Van den Haag quibbles about equality and justice. He attempts to separate them by the use of rhetoric, declaring the importance of justice over equality. But who, without deep consideration of the matter, can unnaturally emphasize one to the exclusion of the other?

Van den Haag tries to justify the abnormal figures for the death sentencing of blacks to the superficial reader with notions of 'distribution.' The term 'distribution' is of no concern to those concerned with the morality or immorality of the death penalty; it is a term which wholly and firmly belongs to the realm of statistics, and as some of us must remind ourselves, defendants are not numbers but human beings.

Van den Haag seems somewhat enamoured by the quantity of the punished rather than the quality of the administering system. He is arguing that the solution to unlawful murder in our society is *lawful* murder in our society! Whichever way you look at it, or whatever terminology proponents use, like the 'distribution of justice,' administering the death penalty is simply revenge, sanctioned by officialdom, with the irreversibility and immutability of the judicial machine working to fulfil its own peculiar notion of justice and its quota of death.

Although, I do not accept the idea of execution as an acceptable form of justice, I do acknowledge the necessity of punishment. Receiving a life sentence in prison, losing one's freedom to do the normal things that everyone takes for granted, like shopping, travelling, meeting friends or sitting on the beach, and knowing year after year that there will never be any freedom, and knowing that the punishment is self-inflicted, is, I feel, a pretty horrid punishment in itself. In addition, what do we gain by executing murderers, besides giving the victim personal satisfaction? What is the real worth of a philosophy whose aim is solely to bring about suffering of the defendant because he or she brought about suffering? Punishing the criminal by death does not heal the injury done to the victim. Neither does the fact that some might feel the criminal deserves execution sanction the implementation of it. No; the idea that execution is a solution is an extremely primitive form of reasoning, and is out of place in a modern, civilised society.

In conclusion, what is most annoying is that we know that the death penalty is cruel, and we know that it is negatively influenced by racial factors, and yet we still cling to this old fashioned form of final torture. Of course prejudice will always be there in one form or another; we cannot eliminate it completely from the judicial system. Maybe we just have to live with it. Living with it, is however, less of a serious problem when the crime involved, and therefore the consequences and sentences, are not severe. The death penalty, as everyone acknowledges - advocates and dissidents alike - is the most severe punishment a defendant can be subjected to. If there be any doubt about fairness, let us evaluate it with all the consideration and sanctity due it.

Maybe executions will always be with us. Just like the old typewriter, perhaps one will find the death penalty lurking in this or that dark corner of the world, waiting to be picked up by some arbitrary demi-god, representing the state, who, going against the sanctity of life, and ignoring the appeal of what his reason and humanity dictate, decides to take the life of the criminal into his own hands. However, it is not only the prosecutor, judge and each of the jury members who decide, it is also the victim. And let us not attempt to escape from the fact that this is a personal decision. The jury, acquiescing to the act of government execution, only gives mild relief to the biting conscience of the judge, prosecutor and victim. Does not this insatiable, distasteful, and downright bizarre appetite for state organized murder reveal more about the nature of the people who perpetuate the system, than about the criminals who are subjected to it? Does not the perpetuation of this assumed right to kill defendants signify our level of civilization? In my view, the only hope for us in realizing our status as true human beings in a real Utopia and discarding our barbarous treatment of defendants must start with the victim taking the first decision not to prosecute. The decision is ultimately his to decide and no one else's. But if he lacks the fortitude to forgive, then he, who at that moment has the power of life over death, forsakes his responsibility to decide personally. Only he perhaps, will not know the true extent his injury has influenced his capacity to reason dispassionately over the future of the defendant; the defendant who has now become the victim's victim, and so he relinquishes his freedom to choose and passes the decision into the hands of the state.

If the victim cannot search within himself and find forgiveness - and I am in no way pretending that such courage comes easily - then the state must show the way and re-evaluate the judicial machinery at work and re-invent its legal and moral values. A failure to act accordingly would only mean that our conception of justice remains nothing more than a disfigured replica of the noble ideal. And such a replica is not one we should keenly boast of, for in abiding by it, we fail in our mission to advance as a civilized race. It is therefore not a true ideal we would espouse, but a distorted one we should conceal with shame.

In light of what we now know, the corridors of the judicial system should be patrolled incessantly by watch-bodies, whose purpose should be to maintain fair play, and offset any racial factors operating in specific cases within the legal system. It is important to push for accountability from *all* quarters. This is the nature of the task before us.

Notes

[1] Bamber Gascoigne, *Encyclopedia of Britain*, (Basingstoke: Macmillan, 1993) 113.
[2] Ernest van den Haag, "The Ultimate Punishment: A Defense," *Contemporary Moral Issues in a Diverse Society*, ed. Julie McDonald (Belmont: Wadsworth, 1998) 247-252.
[3] Gascoigne 537.
[4] Anthony G. Amsterdam, "Race and the Death Penalty," McDonald 265-270.
[5] Erik Eckholm, "Studies Find Death Penalty Tied to Race of the Victims," McDonald 270-273.
[6] Stephen Nathanson, "Does It Matter If the Death Penalty Is Arbitrarily Administered?" McDonald 273-282.

CHAPTER 3

Alternative Vision

The Arab World: Patterns of Utopia

When one looks at Arab history, there appear to be a number of factors which have been a controlling influence on Arab destiny. Such factors may have produced a pattern; but if one does exist it is inextricably linked to a number of chaotic elements. These pattern-forming factors can be fairly simply listed. They are: the religion of Islam - as the legacy of the Prophet's teachings in the form of *The Koran*; the Arabic language, climate, population growth and depletion through plague and famine, trade and navigation, the influx of scientific knowledge from foreign countries - especially those in Europe - and finally, the emergence and collapse of the Ottoman Empire. Although it would at first seem sensible to group them in terms of major and minor forces, with Islam and possibly Arabic belonging to the major class, a close examination of historical events reveals that some of these influences were not continuous over time or dynasties, nor were they applied with constant pressure. Rather they have emerged at various points in the Arabic chronicles like bubbles appearing momentarily on the surface of a swamp, only to quickly lose importance and evaporate once more beneath the surface.

The underlying influences on Arab history

In beginning our examination of the possible patterns of Arabic history, perhaps we should look first at the one thing, after God, which existed before Arabic or even Islam emerged; something which has often been underestimated:

the desert. Ibn Khaldun gives it priority in his preliminary remarks in *The Muqaddimah*, "I have discussed desert civilization first, because it is prior to everything else..."[1] Khaldun believes it is essential to the formation and growth of dynasties. Dynasties, among other things, require both group feeling and an abundance of energy; oddly enough, something only achieved by an abundance of desert. As Khaldun says authoritatively: "As a rule, these things are possible only in connection with desert life. The first stage of dynasties, therefore, is that of desert life."[2] Its importance to the religious life is also noted when Khaldun continues, "The existence of pious men and ascetics is...restricted to the desert..."[3]

Closely allied to the desert is of course the climate. According to Khaldun, the climate of the Arab countries, since they belong to the "three zones," affects the people in the best possible way: "If one pays attention to this sort of thing in the various zones and countries, the influence of the varying quality of the climate upon the character of the inhabitants will become apparent."[4] In other words temperature and climate determine the temperament of peoples.[5] Indeed people who live in hot countries are happy because of the climate. Khaldun says, for instance, that, "The Egyptians are dominated by joyfulness, levity, and disregard for the future."[6]

Arabic and Islam: the backbone of the Arab Utopia

When we go beyond the desert and the climate, which are all natural aspects of geography, the major power of the Arab states has always been Islam and its medium of illumination, the Arabic language. Few would probably argue that religion and language have not been the major influences on culture, identity, economy and literature. This twofold pattern of language and faith has always endured while dynasties have fallen by the wayside. Believers immersed in Islamic learning and the Arabic language have always shared a special bond.

Through the power of the Ottomans, Arabic became more and more important. In Istanbul, Cairo and Damascus, for instance, religion and law were taught in Arabic. Also books relating to religion and law, as well as historical and biographical works, were also printed in Arabic.[7]

Islam was a shared identity which rose above economic, political and individual interests. Even for those whose language was not Arabic, like the Persians and the Turks, there was still the knowledge that they were united in the faith of the Almighty as revealed through the Prophet Muhammad. And it was a faith which flowed out into the community, articulated through the medium of architecture, philosophy and social activity. Also through *The Koran*, a system of law: Islamic law was founded and as this was derived from the revelations of the Prophet in Arabic, ensured a controlling influence on the population. The feast of Ramadan, and especially the pilgrimage to Mecca, were a reminder to Muslims all over the world that they shared a common destiny in this world and automatic salvation in the next one.[8]

Theories of the rise and fall of dynasties

Whereas Islam and Arabic remained a constant force in the history of the Arab nations and their peoples, to dynasties were added an unstable cocktail of population growth and depletion through plague and famine, the influence of trade, the hesitant influx of scientific knowledge from foreign countries; indeed a multiplicity of factors have shaped the nature and life of dynasties. Regarding such dynasties, Hourani and Khaldun have their own theories.

Hourani's hypothesis

Initially, Albert Hourani's explanation seems quite simple. Midway between the termination of the Abbasid Empire and the coming of the Ottoman Empire, dynasties evolved and disintegrated, the pattern repeating itself with endless monotony.[9] Hourani expresses it beautifully: in looking at the possible patterns evident throughout the Arabic chronicles, there is "...what may seem to be the *meaningless* procession of dynasties in Islamic history..."[10] [my italics]. Hourani believes the reason is a combination of the existing dynasty losing its power, while another rival dynasty was able to supersede it because it was stronger. Arabic writers who witnessed the fall and rise of new dynasties attributed the cause to moral deficiencies.[11]

For a dynasty to control all the variables of population: growth, trade, law and order, and the collection of taxes, could only mean success. That is why the Ottoman Empire became so great. The pattern behind the creation of the Ottoman state was one that had occurred many times before. It was a pattern centred around Turkish-derived military might and the enormous advantage that was granted by the advent of gunpowder. The blueprint of Ottoman strength lay in its powerful army, its political system, and its ability to maintain law and order.[12]

Khaldun's hypothesis

Khaldun, on the other hand, has his own systematic explanation of the dynastic paradigm. It is a highly complex one however, which emphasizes the importance of many forces including religion: "Our Prophet wrought no greater miracle than the Koran and the fact that he united the Arabs in his mission...God has united them."[13] For a secure pattern of dynastic growth, religion must engender a context where, "Mutual co-operation and support flourish."[14] Indeed Khaldun notes that religious propaganda imbues a dynasty with legitimate power.

Khaldun believes for any dynasty to materialize, group feeling is required; this is made unnecessary once the dynasty has taken hold. Later, the leaders firmly establish themselves and the people gradually accept them, even if force is an initial prerequisite. In time, the power of the new dynasty expands but is qualified by the border of the lands which constitute it. The dynasty cannot extend further because there is a limit to the people with the same group feeling. Indeed the expansion, power, and duration of a dynasty depends upon the number of its supporters.[15]

For Khaldun, dynasties, like human beings, also have a natural life span so the structure of Arab history is a natural process of birth and death, which is all part of God's plan. As Khaldun declares: "As one can see...[dynasties last]...three generations...In this way, the life span of a dynasty corresponds to the life span of an individual; it grows up and passes into an age of stagnation and thence into retrogression."[16]

Khaldun thinks there are a number of stages involved in the formation of dynasties; stages in which a certain design is apparent. The fifth and final stage seems to be the most important because it is the one where disintegration sets in, and destruction results.[17]

Khaldun as oracle: the fall of the Ottoman Empire.

Khaldun seemed to be able to foretell what would happen to the paradigm of Arabic history many years later, when European power and influence spread through trade and scientific knowledge. A significant part of the population of the new cities was becoming more and more foreign in the 1860-1914 period.[18] Certainly the end of the great Ottoman Empire was heralded by the fact that the Arabic-speaking world came under European rule.[19] It is therefore ironic that in his theory of the rise and fall of dynasties Khaldun notes in a tone which is strangely predictive of future events: "At the end of their power, dynasties eventually resort to employing strangers and accepting them...[these foreigners]...are too recent in origin...the destruction of the dynasty is imminent."[20]

Conclusion

Are there historical patterns behind the Arab Utopia? Undoubtedly yes, although they are in many ways without meaning because of their impermanence. Perhaps others would argue only that *change* is the underlying pattern in Arab history.

Often the effectiveness of a theory is argued in terms of whether it can be used to predict future events. If this is so, Khaldun successfully foretold the end of the Ottoman Empire with his complex hypothesis. However, whereas Khaldun attributes the change in dynasties to a weakening of the moral spirit, I prefer to use the term "human nature." Arab chronicles are far away in time, and therefore our knowledge of them is based on the quality of contemporary records and much speculation regarding the importance of their content. On the other hand, our knowledge of human character is close and familiar.

Khaldun, it seems, believed in the idea of dynasties behaving like living organisms. They are born, they grow, and they reach heights of power and magnificence, but then gradually weaken and die. In other words the coming and going of dynasties reflects the patterns of human growth. It is a natural process which requires little explanation. It is for that reason that an explanation of the dynastic mechanism of Arab history, in terms paralleling the human behavioural and organic system, is probably the most efficacious one.

Notes

[1] Ibn Khaldun, *The Muqaddimah: An Introduction to History*, trans. Franz Rosenthal, Abr. ed. (Princeton: Princeton University Press, 1967) 43.
[2] Khaldun 138.
[3] Khaldun 67.
[4] Khaldun 64.
[5] Khaldun 58.
[6] Khaldun 63.
[7] Albert Hourani, Prologue, *A History of the Arab Peoples*, (New York: Warner Books, 1991) 239.
[8] Hourani 256-57.
[9] Hourani 209.
[10] Hourani 212.
[11] Hourani 209.
[12] Hourani 215.
[13] Khaldun 74.
[14] Khaldun 126.
[15] Khaldun 123-24, 128-30.
[16] Khaldun 136-38.
[17] Khaldun 141-42.
[18] Hourani 297.
[19] Hourani 264.
[20] Khaldun 149.

The Arab World: Dystopia

Following World War Two, many changes took place in the Arab world. Pan-Arabism emerged as a means of forging a separate identity from the West, particularly the superpowers, at a time when the balance of power was changing hands. Arab nationalism was the big force behind Arab politics in the 1950s and 1960s. In Egypt, under the new banner of nationalism, education and the investment of resources became important preoccupations for the regimes following the decline of colonialism.

One of the most important Egyptian nationalist figures of the time was Jamal 'Abd al-Nasir. He wanted Egypt to be independent from America and the USSR, while introducing democratic reforms back home. In addition, the "Muslim Brothers" played an important role in making the Egyptian people aware of the need for independence. So, as we shall see, there were a number of figures and events on the very long road to Egyptian independence and identity. It is an identity which is still relevant to the Arab world today.[1]

The importance and power of Egypt

Much of the political activity was centred in Egypt, particularly Cairo. As Hourani says, "The fact that Cairo was the centre of military and economic decision-making gave an opportunity to the Egyptian government to take the initiative in creating closer links between Arab states."[2] Cairo was also the venue (the other being Alexandria) where the League of Arab States was formed.[3] Even before the Cairo conference of 1945, the city was the British Army's primary base from where they directed their fight for the Middle East during the war.[4]

Anti-colonialism and the fight for independence

Despite Egypt's hope for complete independence following the Second World War, the fact that the country was growing economically meant that like other Arab states, it had to rely on the help of industrialized countries.[5] In truth, because of such dependency, rule under Egyptian leaders was a difficult matter. In addition, Egypt had always been the centre of military power in the Middle East. The British had a base there when fighting the war with Rommel. As Polk says: "...British actions in Egypt...did lend reality to the contention of nationalists that so long as British forces remained on Egyptian soil, Egypt was a good deal less than fully independent."[6]

But apart from the British military, the need for foreign help and investment caused a dependency on those countries the Arab state traded with. The building of the Suez Canal, for example, was undertaken only with the help of strong European backers. Once under the influence of foreign banks, it became difficult for Egypt to break free of the financial commitment it had entered into.[7] The country hurtled towards bankruptcy; and with the country under the supervision of a foreign debt commission, a wave of anti-European feeling understandably swept the country. To complicate matters, the British remained in Egypt dictating public policy to the people.

Understandably, resistance showed itself. It was Saad Zaghlul who led the opposition to the presence of the British, by forming committees all over Egypt whose aim was the end of British rule. The deadlock between Zaghlul and his supporters and the British government continued for many years.[8] It was not until 1954 that most of the British army left Egypt.[9]

Islam and nationalism

Coinciding with a reappraisal of Arab identity came a dissatisfaction with modern life; and in response, modernist voices could be heard who searched for a new type of Islam to meet the growing changes appearing in Arab life. The Egyptian writer Khalid Muhammad Khalid was one of those voices whose message struck a powerful chord.

Khalid argued that the old form of Islam and the freedom of man to think were incompatible.[10] He also criticized its role in maintaining the power of the wealthy while sanctioning the impoverished. In a sense such dissatisfaction and the search for a more humanitarian way of life as that expressed by Khalid was a tentative step in the direction of democracy.

At the same time Mustafa al-Siba'i and others believed in Islam as the supreme moulder of society.[11] And these individuals wanted an Egyptian government which reflected their view point. Again Egypt was the centre of this feeling and it was here that anti-colonialism showed itself.

Following the end of the Second World War, a group known as the "Muslim Brothers," who became a major political influence not only in Egypt but in Syria too, generated a wave of nationalist sentiment. Legitimate pan-Arabic and Islamic forces, as well as elements embracing social equity were clearly evident at this time. As Hourani acutely observes, "The Muslim Brothers were...a movement, particularly in Egypt...[which]...blend[ed] the elements of nationalism, religion and social justice in a more appealing fashion."[12]

Social writers

Egyptian writers like Sayyid Qutb later took up the original cause of the Muslim Brothers. In the *Social Justice in Islam*, Qutb interpreted Islamic teaching in his own way. He felt that Arabs must follow *The Koran* as their guide. Whereas the Egyptian Khalid Muhammad Khalid supported "...the freedom of the intellect..." Qutb in essence stressed the impossibility of freedom because man could not possess something which tied him to this world.[13]

'Abd Al-Nasir, pan-Arabism and "democratic Marxism"

Another movement that emerged at the time was the one led by 'Abd al-Nasir. It initially had no policies and little in the way of ideology except for promising the people - including the peasant masses - a regime that stressed Arab identity. For Nasir and his followers Arab unity was more important than political parties and factions. Later, as the regime developed, so did an ideology that became synonymous with the personality of Nasir himself.[14]

Clearly, Nasir's strength lay in his understanding that the Arab world was changing, and so he tried to tailor Islam to suit the times. Although Nasir considered Islam as an important Arab social and spiritual bond, pan-Arabism became the central element in his philosophy.[15]

Although each Arab state had its own separate culture, Egyptian governments prior to Nasir had always stressed group identity when dealing with foreign nations; no one Arab state being more important than another. Now however, Nasir wanted Egypt to be the prime negotiator in Arab policy making.[16] Nasir's "Arab socialism" was a diluted form of Marxist ideology, with a capitalist element thrown in. The tenet of the regime was the expression of, "freedom, socialism and unity...[where]...Freedom means that of the country and of the citizen."[17] What Nasir's movement was offering was democracy - Arab style. There was to be no inequality of gender; and education and health care were to benefit everyone. In addition, pan-Arabism should be democratic too: there was to be equality between all Arab nations - providing Cairo could be the centre of all policy making.[18]

If we assess the veracity and power of the regime through the Arab Socialist Union, however, it did not cater to the true democratic right of expression, and forbade any form of dissent. The Muslim Brothers accused it of using Islam to hide its real political ideology. And despite the Marxist contribution to the Nasir regime, true Marxists dismissed it for not being "real socialism." From a pan-Arab perspective, however, the policies of Nasir - as well as the man himself - were held in high regard.[19]

The influence of Marxism

Despite the influence of Marxist ideology on the policies of Nasir, Marxism developed separately in Egypt through the unavoidable influence of Chinese and Soviet communism.

Initially Marxism filtered into society through language. As Hourani says: "it was shown in the articulation of Marxist ideas in Arabic. Once more, the centre of this activity was Egypt." From this time on Egyptian history became interwoven with Marxist philosophy. Those regimes that encouraged the people to support them because of national interests rather than the parties were seen as pursuing selfish goals.[20]

However, if we evaluate its merits at the peak of its success, what emerged was a package of state-owned and driven production, fairness of income distribution, a fair taxation system and decent social services. It was a time when an independent, democratic, religious, Marxist, nationalist and anti-colonialist play of forces were all at work together. The anti-colonialist sentiment, again centred in Egypt, was led by the communist movement, which in spite of being made of separate factions, gave support to those who were opposing the British after the Second World War.[21]

What was the major factor in delaying Egyptian independence for so long? Was it anti-colonialism, democracy, Islam, Marxism, or pan-Arabism which prevented Egypt from becoming free? Personally, I would say it was a combination of Islam and the bullying behaviour of the British as demonstrated by the "...use [of] their military power to impose upon the Egyptians a prime minister of their choosing."[22] But there was one other crucial factor: the Arab psyche. Certainly through Islam the Egyptian people were spiritually independent. Or were they? As Hourani notes, "Islam...[Khalid Muhammad Khalid]...asserted, was a religion of reaction, attacking the freedom of the human intellect..."[23] Perhaps their obedience to religion deprived the Egyptian people of the strength and spirit to resist all external forces: British or otherwise. Perhaps they became too servile to accept anything other than foreign rule. Even Polk seems to suggest something similar when he says:

> ...I believe part of the explanation may lie elsewhere: in what may be called the psychology of development. The Egyptians had become accustomed to having others make their decisions and were so often told that they were weak [and] inefficient...that they almost stopped aspiring to what may be the most crucial of all elements in the developmental process, the ability to work with and trust one another.[24]

But Polk is also saying here that there was a lack of cooperation and unity. But is that surprising? As Hourani observes, according to many, "...social justice could be achieved only under the leadership of a government which took Islam as the basis of its policy and laws."[25] If this is the case, British jurisdiction in Egypt certainly failed to meet this requirement.

Was it merely because of the forces implicated above that Egyptian independence was so long in coming? Is not the never-ending struggle to find an answer to that question the real "...ghost which has haunted successive generations of Egyptians up to the present time?"[26]

Notes

[1] Albert Hourani, Prologue, *History of the Arab Peoples* By Hourani (New York: Warner Books, 1991) 351.
[2] Hourani 355.
[3] Hourani 355-356.
[4] Hourani 355.
[5] Hourani 377.
[6] William R. Polk, *The Arab World Today* (London: Harvard UP, 1991) 143.
[7] Polk 136.
[8] Polk 138-141.
[9] Polk 186.
[10] Hourani 397.
[11] Hourani 398.
[12] Hourani 403.
[13] Hourani 398.
[14] Hourani 405.
[15] Hourani 406.
[16] Hourani 406.
[17] Hourami 406.
[18] Hourani 406-407.
[19] Hourani 407.
[20] Hourani 402.
[21] Hourani 401, 403.
[22] Polk 186.
[23] Hourani 397.
[24] Polk 142.

[25] Hourani 398.
[26] Polk 142-143.

CHAPTER 4

Some Theoretical Considerations of Utopia

Universal Communication

English, as we are readily starting to realise, is becoming the dominant language of the world. At the present time there are somewhere between 4,000 and 5,000 languages used around the world.[1] English speakers however, are everywhere. Every continent has at least 300 million native speakers of the language; another 250 million plus speakers also exist for whom English is a second language. In addition, another sixth of the world's population use English in social circumstances.[2] As Peter Newmark says:

> English has triumphed where Esperanto failed, and become the international language. Given that it is financially so rewarding, all the national establishments and a vastly increased number of working people are going to know English.[3]

And so it appears the use of English is growing still. Apart from business, English is now officially used in aviation circles as well as in the world of rock music. 6 out of 10 radio programmes are now broadcast in English, and 7 out of 10 letters are now sent in English.

Considering that 400 years ago, English was little more than a dialect, the position it holds today is quite amazing.[4] There is no doubt that part of the reason for the stronghold of English is due to the colonies where English speakers took with them their language and culture and seeded them in their new worlds. In addition to those who emigrated and thus took English to the colonies, from a practical point of view, it paid to continue to use English for daily commerce. We must not forget that there were 845 distinct languages in use in the sub-continent and it would have been impossible to maintain an effective administration without a standardized form of communication.

In India the position of English was sustained through a severe crisis of linguistic identity. The Central Government decided back in 1950 that the official language was going to be Hindi - unsurprising as there were 65 million speakers of the language. Riots and deaths ensued and it was only after the *Shastri* government realised the strength of feeling regarding English, that the language was given partner-status along with Hindi as an official language. Again, from a practical angle, West Africa has a plethora of languages which can in no way bring about efficient understanding in business and daily life if anything other than a single language is used for communication. In Nigeria for instance, 400 languages are used. In countries like Ghana and Nigeria, English is thus considered the official language. In twenty-nine countries, English is now the national language, and in another fifteen countries it is the official language.[5]

So, the use of English is increasing and what has enforced the trend is the development of technology in countries where English is widely in use. English it seems, is the most efficacious language for describing complex technology with its plethora of apt terminology. It is also the foremost scientific language with most research papers now being written in English. In addition most radio and television programmes are now presented in English, and people have become more and more familiar with the language through the music industry.[6]

The universal language of Utopia

Will there be a single language of Utopia in the future? Will citizens of the world speak "Utopian?" Interestingly, the *Baha'i Faith* - a religious group founded in Iran by *Baha'u'llah* in 1852 - promotes the requirement for a single language which will bring people together and serve all administrative purposes.[7] Although to the best of my knowledge, nothing is explicitly stated in the Baha'i literature, English, Baha'is' propose, is this language:

> ...there needs to be selected either an existing or an artificial language to serve as an international auxiliary language, which would be taught in every school throughout the world alongside the native language and literature of that country.[8]

It is clear that one language is needed for truly global communication to take place, and it seems that English is slowly becoming this language.

In his article "Global economy, global language" Michael Hindley discusses in depth, the rising importance of the English language and the response of the rest of the world to its escalating significance in world affairs. Hindley says: "The simple answer to the question 'Is there going to be a global language?' would be 'yes.' It is going to be English of a sort."[9]

Other linguistic contenders

It is difficult to visualize any other languages other than English being the dominant language of the future. Having said that, through an attempt to entice people to learn their language and partly through a process of natural evolvement, certain countries will simplify their own language. Space precludes an in-depth analysis of many of the world's languages, but three or four will suffice to demonstrate the process that will inevitably take place.

The German language

As many people know, the German language has three genders, "der," "die" and "das." As any student of the language will tell you, remembering when to use which gender is not a simple business. Now many of the students of German are told by their teachers to try to memorize the noun along with its gender. According to *The Collins German Pocket Dictionary* for example, "These genders are largely unpredictable, and you just have to learn them as a feature to be remembered with each word."[10]

However, no matter what linguistic pedagogues might say, there is no good practical reason why there is a need to have three genders. If there were only one gender, the language would not fall apart, but would simply become more efficient and user-friendly. It *will* happen that the written differences between the genders will eventually disappear - through official sanction - with the use of a *single* article being the order of the day; but first this will be preceded by verbal extinction through non-observance. That is to say, people will simply stop using all the genders in everyday conversation, and native listeners will not care and eventually not notice. It already happens now with foreign speakers of English. Many Russian speakers of English simply omit all articles when they converse in English. Poor German speakers of English tend to pronounce the definite article "the" as a kind of "zur" sound. Some French speakers often pronounce the definite article simply as "d." The same thing is bound to happen with German in the distant future; but it will not only be poor speakers of German who do this, but eventually the Germans, the Swiss and the Austrians themselves. And it will not be wisdom that will bring this about: that is to say the Germans, realizing themselves that having three genders is both troublesome and unnecessary; no, not a willingness on their part, but simple neglect by non-native users.

Interestingly, related ideas are evident in the article, "The endless stairway of language" by Professor Jean Atchinson, who examines the way language has developed in man, and reviews the opinions of various language experts, coming to the conclusion that, "...language was essentially chaotic, and then neatened itself up - though never entirely."[11] I firmly believe the neglect talked about earlier will become habit-forming with a new developing system of rules in German, which will mirror somewhat the original development of language generally. As Atchinson says, "Unstructured word sequences were probably found, with quite a lot of repetition, though with some ordering preferences. Then preferences become habits, and the habits potentially become 'rules'."[12] The process may be summarized as follows: 1. preferences - 2. habits - 3. rules. Atchinson continues with some very plausible arguments as to how linguistic preferences turn into habit-forming phrases. For example, newspaper headlines often contain phrases that omit grammar, and yet do not preclude understanding.[13]

At the beginning, this process will be simply user-friendly and unofficial, but as the new spoken system becomes more and more widespread, so will language-bodies and governments come to recognise the new status of the language. They will have to, as the magnitude of dissenting speakers will overcome any official resistance.

However, as the Germans realize that the popularity and practicality of their own language is slowly diminishing, they will attempt to draw students to the study of their language by officially sanctioned simplification; however, by that time, it will be too late. Jean Atchinson says of languages generally, "The danger is not that any language system will break down but that some languages will fall into disuse."[14] Where I disagree with Atchinson, is the breaking down of languages; it will happen with German: it will break down *and* fall into disuse. Some sense this even now. Recently, the Germans have felt that their language is becoming marginalized. The German politicians who attend meetings at the European parliament are becoming increasingly irritated at the way in which English and French are being allowed to become the prominent languages. There was a time when many German diplomats were proud of their English abilities and insisted, almost to the point of irritation, on using English, especially to other English diplomats and especially to the media. Now there is definitely a trend in the opposite direction.[15]

The Chinese language

Chinese is, like Japanese, one of those languages that uses pictorial characters to express concrete and abstract ideas in script. There is a need for a tremendous number of characters in the Chinese writing system as there is a plethora of homonyms in the language, which though possible to differentiate aurally because of the tone system, nevertheless necessitates the use of a vast number of these characters to represent all the ideas the average literate Chinese would wish to express. According to Kan Qian, there are over 50,000 characters in existence with around three thousand or so necessary to achieve a moderate level of literacy.[16] Now if we compare this to the 26 letters in the English alphabet, it does not require a high degree of intellect to see that learning all those characters, even if possible by the dedicated Chinese language student, is extremely laborious, but more importantly, grossly inefficient.

Although there are more people who speak Chinese than English, the linguistic variety of Chinese even for native speakers can create problems. As Broughton et al comment, "...[Chinese] is effectively six mutually unintelligible dialects little used outside China."[17]

Even though many economists predict that China will be a major world player in the 21st and 22nd centuries, this does not necessarily mean that the position of its language will strengthen. Of course, not everyone agrees on the certainty of China's economic rise anyway. Walter Long says:

> China is changing with exponential rapidity. Now 'China is back,' as they say, plus devouring everything modern in pragmatic Chinese fashion, with philosophy subordinated to economics. How it will turn out is anybody's guess, and any person or text claiming to know with certainty should be regarded with suspicion.[18]

At any rate, if we assume that the Chinese economic miracle does occur with its long and slow course to a rich world power from its present status as just a world power, the rest of the world may be forced to recognize the importance of the Chinese language. However, even if it does become strong economically, people will not on the whole be willing to learn the language because of its difficulty. Of course there will always be groups of dedicated enthusiasts who will be quite willing to spend years of their free time studying all those 50,000 odd characters; but knowing human nature for what it is, people will not be bothered. People will always choose the path of least resistance, which in language terms means they will opt for the easiest language to learn and the easiest way to learn it, or at worst, not learn any language at all. However, before we feel completely rest assured that the demise of Chinese will take place, it is important to consider another factor - that of *pinyin* transliteration.

In an attempt to simplify the language somewhat, the Chinese government, introduced what is known as *pinyin*, a quite marvellous and simple transliteration of the language using roman letters; a system whose roots may be traced to the pioneer Lu Zhuangzhang (1854-1928).[19] Tone changes, inherent in the language, are indicated by marks above the vowel of the syllable; this together with the use of Roman letters means the need to learn vast numbers of Chinese characters is obviated.[20]

Although for the student beginning the study of the Chinese language such a system is really a gateway to being able to communicate in the language, there is an aesthetic problem for those whose studies reach beyond the elementary level. In the case of the French language for example, people enjoy French because they can read Sartre or Voltaire, or whoever is one's preference in the original French. The problem with Chinese however is that there is no literature in *pinyin*. If the Chinese government increasingly wants people to take up their language, they must recognise that there is a need for *pinyin* literature because part of the reason why people enjoy a foreign language apart from communicating directly with the foreign people who speak it, is the opportunity to read the philosophical, historical and political literature of the language they are studying. Even if the Chinese do bring about such a change - which will take considerably more effort than the German government did to revise the German spelling system several years ago - they will fail in their efforts to disseminate the language abroad; but their endeavour will perhaps be of benefit to their own people in terms of the simplification of the learning and use of their own language.

Eventually however, despite the Chinese people's attempt at clinging to their language, certainly, in its present form at any rate, it will eventually disappear. The only hope for Chinese is if the number of speakers using the language increases - which is certainly happening at the present time - but also, only if those speakers emigrate with their new universally accepted *pinyin* language and export it to other countries, like the English did in the colonies of the past. If the number of Chinese communities builds up over time in many different countries, and we have a truly global Chinese population, then the *pinyin* form of the Chinese language will flourish.

The Japanese language

"We shall require," said Japanese Prime Minister General Tojo during the Second World War, "large numbers of English speakers to administer our conquered territories. In Australia alone the figure will be enormous." He was of course responding to extremists in the press who wanted all teaching of the enemy language English throughout Japan to come to a stop. According to Foreign Office adviser John Morris, General Tojo thought, "...that it would be many years before the people of those territories could acquire a sufficient knowledge of Japanese to make the use of English no longer necessary." [21] Tojo - who was later hanged by the allies for war crimes - was of course severely mistaken in his view that Japanese would one day become the language taught to the *enemy* through its own military victory and defeat of American military forces.

The worm, as they say, has indeed turned, for although Japan is considered to be the economic leader of Asia, its language will eventually fall into decline; indeed the future of the Japanese language is more uncertain than the Chinese language, for at least China has the advantage of size; Japan however, is a small country that has never achieved the export of its language beyond its own borders.

In the same way as the Germans and the Chinese will severely modify their languages as they realize that they will one day become obsolete, so too will the Japanese attempt to do something about the complexity of their own language.

Like Chinese, there are according to Roy Andrew Miller, 48,902 kanji, although only (only!) 2,000 or so are required to read a newspaper.[22] Also in Japanese, there are other characters known as *hiragana* and *katakana* - the former used in grammatical constructions together with kanji, while the latter, katakana is used for foreign words and phrases.[23] There is no practical reason why foreign words cannot be expressed in *hiragana*; its use is merely a matter of custom, so this will probably be the first part of the language to become obsolete. Then there is the problem of *kanji*: despite the introduction of the *Toyo Kanji* ("Kanji for practical use") introduced by the Japanese government in 1946, it is still a troublesome and inefficient system.[24]

Like Chinese, the *idea* of representing objects and concepts by characters rooted in pictures appears a good one, though it is totally impractical. The Japanese themselves know, and will freely admit that having to learn *kanji* is extremely troublesome. And one of the things that aids the learning of the language is the repetitive writing of the correct *kanji* stroke order. Now, as everyone knows, most people are using computers to type almost everything these days, handwritten letters are fast becoming a thing of the past. As Japanese type more and more in their business and private life, a time will come when they no longer write anything at all, and therefore will not practise writing the written strokes. When that happens, their competency at reading, and especially at writing *kanji*, will decrease. The Japanese government may well introduce a new form of the language to compensate for this deficiency. The last time they did that was when they introduced the *Toyo Kanji* back in 1946. This was in effect an official introduction of simplified *kanji*. Before this, people often could not read the newspapers because there was so much complicated *kanji*. Roy Andrew Miller says that in 1927, the Tokyo newspapers were using between 7,500 and 8,000 *kanji*.[25] Indeed, even after the introduction of the new *kanji*, many people had been so used to using the old forms that they continued to do so, signifying the reluctance of Japanese to accept change, especially when it concerns their language.

However strong the initial power of governmental and popular resistance, I predict that in the long run, both Japanese, Chinese, Korean and all other Asian languages will go the same way as Latin: they will become nothing more than academic curiosities with no practical value.

The French language

There is no doubt that one of the attractions of the French language is the beauty of its spoken "music." Asking whether French will fall by the wayside and eventually become extinct is like asking if Mozart will ever die in the hearts of those who appreciate the perfect splendour of classical music. However, leaving sentimentality behind, it seems clear that in no way can French become a dominant language; and certainly decision-making bodies in Britain today, who believe that language learning should be limited to French, are mistaken. As David Graddol says, "We certainly need to equip our children with skills beyond statutory French."[26]

Having said that, Michael Hindley believes that English will be the dominant language of the world - excluding Europe, which he suggests will be bi-lingual at the insistence of the French. As he declares: "English may be the language of the world, but it will not be the language of Europe - or only over the dead body of the French Language."[27]

Will the English language also change?

All languages change over time and undoubtedly, so will English. In his article "Global economy, global language" Michael Hindley discusses in depth, the rising importance of the English language and the response of the rest of the world to its ascension. Hindley says: "The simple answer to the question 'Is there going to be a global language?' would be 'yes.' It is going to be English of a sort."[28] What Hindley means by this is that there will not be only one type of English. For example, recently in America, it appears that California has decided that Black ghetto dialogue is a proper language and may now be taught as one.[29]

English will become diverse in many respects; it will gradually become more and more separated from the original. As Hindley says: "Interestingly, the English are, more and more, losing control of English."[30] This seems very true as it is predicted that gradually more non-native speakers of English will overshadow the number of native speakers who use the language.[31]

In his article "A single language for Europe" Pierre Dupont reflects on the importance of both the French and the English languages in Europe, but suggests that English could well be the dominant language:

> In time, who knows, there may even be a federal language which...could be English. If it were, it would be a new form of English, a Eurolect called 'European English,' moulded over a number of decades by the several needs of the member states' inhabitants, by their cultures, languages, legislation, administration and translations. It would probably be to us what Chaucer's English would have been to King Harold's Anglo-Saxon! It would certainly not be the language of the British Isles as we know it today.[32]

In an article entitled "What's the future for languages?" David Graddol agrees that the way English has become the leading language of the world, "Is one of the most striking phenomena of the 20th century."[33] However, he warns that while many English people therefore consider it unnecessary to learn foreign languages, world communication will not be based only on English, but a variety of languages. He argues that people will need to speak several languages.[34] What Graddol fails to recognise however, is that 1) although people who speak the difficult languages like Chinese and Arabic for example, will continue to speak them in private, they will not use them in business or international travel, simply because nobody else will be familiar with them; 2) the predictability of human nature: to take Arabic and Chinese as examples once more, Arabic will not prosper beyond its use in Arab countries and neither will native speakers of Chinese take the language beyond its Chinese borders, because ultimately people will refuse to learn these languages because of their difficulty and because of the connotations of their politically harsh regimes; 3) finally, Graddol fails to take into account good old fashioned convenience. Why should we have a plethora of incompatible language mediums when we only need one - English? However, just because of course, one only needs a single global language, does not mean that it will be English; only that the chances that it will be another language will be exceedingly small considering the secure position that English already has around the world today. Of course Graddol is also not taking into account the United States. One primary force behind globalizing English is the Americans who through trade are slowly trying to entice the whole world into joining the drive towards economic wealth.[35]

One of the ways English will change is through the influence of computing and the internet which has virtually monopolized the English language with 8 out of 10 per cent of all software programmes now in English.[36]

Another thing that seems to be occurring at the moment with computing is that senders of e-mail are dropping capital letters from the words used in their messages. If this trend continues - which it undoubtedly will because using lower case letters saves time when operating any computer keyboard quickly - capitalization may disappear all together. For quite some considerable time, officialdom will attempt to keep grammatical etiquette in what they believe is its rightful place of importance, but gradually the dropping of capital letters will be seen to be the norm. Again, like in the case of genders in German, neglect will be the underlying force behind such linguistic evolution.

Interestingly, omission in language has always existed and we can see how the drive towards efficiency causes a tendency towards preference, then habit, and then finally to a rule-bound system. Observe the following:

"FURNITURE FACTORY PAY CUT RIOT"
"MISSING ENVOY RIDDLE DRAMA"
"MORE EARTHQUAKE DEATHS"

English Newspapers are famous for using language in their headlines that omits articles, and yet every native speaker can readily understand what the subsequent article is about. This form of language is not used for aesthetic reasons but purely in order to save space; it is the drive for efficiency talked about before and which, in the end, controls the development of all language.[37]

It does not seem unreasonable therefore to accept the prediction that English will undergo such changes of refinement and efficiency in the far off future. It may be that another language does become more popular, or simply more necessary than English because there are more speakers of it, as is now the case with Chinese; or simply because it is more efficient. And we must remember that efficiency will always override aesthetic tastes - or to put it another way the inherent beauty of languages will become subservient to convenience. And anyway, beauty has always been a personal thing; convenience has not. For example, other languages, though very strange sounding may have been more efficient than English. Dean Farr, writing in 1865 asked: "What shall we say...of the Yamparico, who speaks a sort of gibberish like the growling of a dog? Of Fuegians, whose language is an inarticulate clucking?"[38]

Perhaps a new language will be specially developed, like Esperanto and Korean was, but this time for global use; a new artificial language which is more effective than anything we now use on earth. In any case, whatever language we do decide to use for global communication in our 21st century Utopia, will Shakespearean verse ever sound the same again?

Notes

[1] Geoffrey Broughton, Christopher Brumfit, Roger Flavell, Peter Hill and Anita Pincas, *Teaching English as a Foreign Language* (2nd Ed. London: Routledge & Kegan Paul, 1981) 1.
[2] Broughton 1.
[3] Peter Newmark, "Paragraphs on Translation - 49," *The Linguist: Journal of the Institute of Linguists* 92.
[4] Broughton 1.
[5] Broughton 2-3.
[6] Broughton 3.
[7] Joseph Sheppherd, *The Elements of The Baha'i Faith*, (Dorset: Element, 1992) 29.
[8] Sheppherd 74.
[9] Michael Hindley, "Global economy, global language," *The Linguist: Journal of the Institute of Linguists* 66.
[10] Veronika Schnorr, Ute Nicole and Peter Terrell, *The Collins German Pocket Dictionary* (London: Collins, 1988).419
[11] Jean Atchinson, "The endless stairway of language," *The Linguist* 36 (1997): 176.
[12] Atchinson 176.
[13] Atchinson 176.
[14] Atchinson 177.
[15] Hindley 67.
[16] Kan Qian, *Colloquial Chinese: A Complete Language Course* (London: Routledge, 1996) 11.
[17] Broughton 1.
[18] Walter Long, *Finger-Tip Chinese* (New York: Weatherhill, 1996) 14.

[19] John DeFrancis, Ed. *ABC Chinese-English Dictionary* (St. Leonards: Allen & Unwin, 1997) vi.
[20] Walter Long 12.
[21] John Morris, *Traveller From Tokyo* (Liverpool: Penguin, 1946) 86.
[22] Roy Andrew Miller, Ed. *A Japanese Reader: Graded Lessons for Mastering the Written Language* (4th ed., Rutland: Charles E. Tuttle, 1992) 14.
[23] Miller 23-32.
[24] Miller 13.
[25] Miller 14.
[26] Graddol "What's the future for languages?" *The Linguist* 37 (1998) 146.
[27] Hindley 67.
[28] Hindley 66.
[29] Hindley 66.
[30] Hindley 66.
[31] Hindley 66
[32] Pierre Dupont "A single language for Europe?" *The Linguist* 37 (1998) 165.
[33] Graddol 144.
[34] Graddol 144.
[35] Hindley 66.
[36] Hindley 66.
[37] Michael Swan, *Practical English Usage* (Oxford: Oxford U.P., 1989) 409.
[38] Atchinson 177.

Controlling the Individual

Is fate in our own hands or in the hands of the gods? This is a question which has preoccupied philosophers since the time of Plato and Socrates. If the latter is the case, then destiny is out of our hands. If the former is the case, then is it possible to influence and even become master over behaviour in order to achieve positive interaction among people and nations, thereby ensuring a stress-free, peaceful environment, i.e. Utopia?

B.F. Skinner believes that man himself can determine his own behaviour through techniques acquired in the field of behaviourist psychology. His use of the term "human conditioning" refers to a system of training people to behave in ways sanctioned by those inventing and conducting the training programme.[1]

Behaviourist psychology has a long experimental tradition and whatever one's views of the efficaciousness and morality of the application of behaviourist principles, few would argue that for such a systematic policy of influencing people's behaviour to be really comprehensive and therefore truly effective, a human conditioning programme would have to start when human beings are in their infancy, precisely because children are not adults; adults tend to question authority, seeking justification for the rules and treatment the state subjects them to. Children on the other hand, tend not to question those who govern them; the flexibility and openness of their minds can be taken advantage of by educationalists for example, in order that a successful level of intellectual achievement can be effected, guaranteeing them a proper place in society when they grow into adults.

However, the idea that training people's minds and behaviour is a wholly good one and beneficial to those undergoing it is false. One only has to look at present day communist North Korea to see that small children are deleteriously affected by the communist regime's brainwashing education system. Children are exposed only to the tenets of the regime led by a dictator who enforces a policy of non-exposure to democratic and free principles.

In B. F. Skinner's book, *Walden Two*, the whole debate is presented in the form of a novel where the main characters in the story represent the different sides of the argument. Castle is the opponent attempting to verbally counteract Frazier's arguments for the justification of the Walden Two conditioning agenda specifically, and the philosophy underlying the society in general. Frazier's initial comments on the need for the Walden Two Utopian state reflect a fairly pragmatic reasoning: when Frazier says of the people who make up society, "Each of us has interests which conflict with the interest of everybody else. That's our original sin and it can't be helped."[2] So for Frazier, there is a basic flaw in the human-societal system; a flaw which cannot be corrected once in evidence. The only way Frazier can offset negative behavioural outcomes stemming from this flaw is by creating a society which neutralizes the private, selfish desires of the individual from birth. Particularly repulsive to Castle is the toleration training.[3] Personally, I find the results of the training programme of interest, but I agree with the Castle character that the methodology seems severe and harsh; the anecdote of the soup does seem a "...display of sadistic tyranny."[4]

However, Frazier's arguments sometimes seem convincing, as for example when he compares the effectiveness of the nineteenth century English public school system in producing "...crops of brave men...," and Walden Two, where "...every man [is] a brave man."[5]

But what about creativity and inventiveness? If behaviour was controlled completely, how would man create with his mind? Everything we have in the world that is man-made has only been possible because of the capriciousness of discovery and through unrestrained intellectual and behavioural processes. For creativity to happen man must be free to use his intellect to think up ways of doing things, and to solve problems which would always exist, despite the miracles of technology and the effectiveness of Frazier's conditioning programme. Without creativity, no new discoveries would be made and mankind could not advance or adapt. Adaption has been the key to man's success at surviving in the world, battling against all that fate has thrown at him, and winning. Without the ability to adapt, man would surely die out like the dinosaurs of long ago.

Such a society as Walden Two would be self-perpetuating. And no one would be in a position to question the authority and criticize the morality and lawfulness of that society because no one would be exempt from conditioning; the only potential critics would be internal to the system, inextricably a part of it, and thus, through that same conditioning, would only be able to pay tribute to its merits. And those conditioned to operate in the society would be like animals performing in a circus.

To borrow partly Joseph Wood Krutch's expression for a moment: the idea of creating a better society of contented individuals who can interact without the forces of conflicting interests coming into play is a noble one, but such a Utopia is achieved by an ignoble means; a system which works at the terrifying expense of personal freedom and volition.[6] As Robert Blatchford says, it is much better to use reason if we want to try and convince a man to do something, rather than use brute force or punishment.[7] Of course habit and custom purloin our freedom, and negative emotions like jealousy, prejudice and hate do occur and interfere with our conduct as rational beings; but at the end of the day, is it not our ability to reason in spite of our dark side that defines us uniquely as human beings?

If I consider the extremes of determinism and libertarianism, I remain unconvinced of the absolute veracity of neither because I will never be able to prove which is true and to what degree it is true.

Is the whole question of whether free will exists or not a purely semantic problem, as the soft determinist W. T. Stace believes?[8] According to the tenets of soft determinism, a mixture of determinism and free will is involved in human behaviour.[9] To a certain extent behaviour is predetermined, but choice plays its part too. For example, you go to the cinema on a Sunday because your parents took you as a child and because you like the cinema and because you cannot go any other day because you are working; but in the end you still have the choice of whether to go or not. If the film showing on Sunday is not one that appeals to you then you may choose not to go of your own free will, in spite of the large probability of your going because previous experience, habit, and hereditary factors dictate it.

This notion of choosing or using one's free will needs to be differentiated from instances where we cannot exercise our volition. Behaviour occurring as a result of our free will is caused by our personal desires and wishes. Behaviour which, on the other hand, is not free, is brought about because of some external factor in which we had no choice in being affected by it. The behaviour of the citizens of Walden Two would, therefore, fall under the latter category, because although they would choose to do the right thing all the time, the cause would be based on external factors, i.e. conditioning and reinforcement, thereby eliminating free will. Or to put it another way, free will would be an illusion only, without any basis in reality.

But one thing is certain, though I can never know if freedom is real or was settled in some divine way before I was born, I cannot escape, however hard I try, from the intuitive *feeling* that I am free and in that respect my opinion corresponds with that of Corliss Lamont.[10] In addition, as W. T. Stace says, although professors of philosophy believe in the supremacy of determinism, in their everyday lives, "...they behave as if they and others were free."[11] For example, if a student does not turn up for a lecture or fails to hand in an essay on time, then the professor will not react as if it was already determined that the student was going to behave in that way and subsequently behave as if there is no problem; the professor will react as if the student freely chose not to go to class or not to do the essay. What the professor advocates in the classroom and what he instinctively feels is very different. What we can conclude from this is that predictability and free will are able to coexist.

But if we do accept freedom as the true cause of human behaviour, then we have to consider the importance of personal responsibility in human affairs, particularly crime. If there were no such thing as freedom, then how could we have a legal system and accuse criminals of bad behaviour when what they did was already determined beforehand? After all, they could not have done anything differently. And how could we label people good or bad when all they did was obey the fate they were programmed to obey? Does this then mean that it is wrong to punish criminals for their wrongdoings? No, because by punishing them there is the chance - especially if the punishment is more rehabilitative than punitive - that the person's behaviour will be changed and that they will think twice before committing such acts again in the future. Also of course, other potential criminals may be discouraged from doing similar criminal behaviour.

There is also the point about the possibility of certain vocabulary being rendered obsolete if there is no free will;

and it is an interesting point at that. If someone offers us a cigarette, how can we use the word "accept" to denote our consent to taking it? Acceptance indicates choice and also the winning over of its opposite, refusal; but if there is no volition then we would have to use special determinist vocabulary like "*as programmed* I took the cigarette." This scenario would entail a complete linguistic paradigm shift. Indeed, morality too would become an obsolete concept as people would automatically behave in a manner that is sanctioned by society.

The other thing that would become obsolete would of course be the government. There would be no need for all the various governmental institutions and departments that we have now. Initially, a Walden Two type society would require a small group of scientists to start and maintain the programme; eventually, however, this group would become one leader; but later on, once the society had been programmed to function independently of man, the Frazier role would become obsolete.[12] And with the disappearance of the original elite God-scientists, would disappear any lust for power. All the successors would be conditioned until there would be no need for individuals to maintain the system; society would become one whole, organic and unthinking, automatic machine.

If free will exists then we are directly responsible for everything we do - good or bad. We therefore cannot escape our own moral responsibility. It offers us, by way of our intellect, the opportunity to choose right from wrong. If God's purpose is that men must live on earth and be tested constantly by having to face the two alternatives of right or wrong, then a society like Walden Two, with its human conditioning programme, would take away our chance to overcome evil, and using our God-given reason, hopefully make the right, sinless choice. A religious theorist could argue, and rightly so, that to engineer such a society would be to go against the wishes of the Creator. If God wanted us to be mere puppets he would have given us strings. I personally do not want to be robbed of my mind, the beauty of choice, my independence of will, my humanness; in a word: my soul. Perhaps in the future we will not have to worry about freedom, determinism and moral responsibility at all because man will become more skilful at determining what is right and wrong more easily, and become more adept at understanding why certain acts are undesirable (irrespective of the level of his own intellect), and will correct his own negative impulses before they transform themselves into criminal modes of behaviour. Maybe as Clarence Darrow believed, criminal behaviour - in the case of theft, for example - is only a result of financial need; if this need was satisfied, if more charity were to appear, then perhaps criminal behaviour would disappear.[13] And if criminal behaviour were to disappear, a term like "morality" would become a totally obsolete concept. The ramification of course would be that a society without crime would be a happy one. That would be the real Utopia, and the need to change people's behaviour to maintain only positive outcomes would become redundant.

In conclusion, I believe that our behaviour is determined by the influence of various subconscious factors as a result of previous experiences along with their positive or negative outcomes, hereditary factors, knowledge of the situation and also a measure of natural instinct regarding the probability of various outcomes and their consequences for the person once the act is committed. Perhaps then, we should follow the relative determinism of Corliss Lamont. And yet of all the factors influencing behaviour, hereditary and environment, I believe, are the chief factors which most have an effect on, and determine behaviour; hence my committal to Robert Blatchford's view.

Notes

[1] B.F. Skinner, "Walden Two," John R. Burr, and Milton Goldinger. *Philosophy and Contemporary Issues.* 7th ed. (New Jersey: Prentice Hall, 1996) 56, 59, 62, 66-67.
[2] B.F. Skinner 55.
[3] B.F. Skinner 57-9.
[4] B. F. Skinner 57.
[5] B.F. Skinner 61.
[6] Joseph Wood Krutch, "Ignoble Utopias," John R. Burr, and Milton Goldinger. *Philosophy and Contemporary Issues.* 7th ed. (New Jersey: Prentice Hall, 1996) 70.
[7] Robert Blatchford, "The Delusion of Free Will," John R. Burr, and Milton Goldinger. *Philosophy and Contemporary Issues.* 7th ed. (New Jersey: Prentice Hall, 1996) 42.
[8] W.T. Stace, "The Problem of Free Will," John R. Burr, and Milton Goldinger. *Philosophy and Contemporary Issues.* 7th ed. (New Jersey: Prentice Hall, 1996) 47.
[9] W.T. Stace 47-54.
[10] Corliss Lamont, "Freedom of Choice and Human Responsibility," John R. Burr, and Milton Goldinger. *Philosophy and Contemporary Issues.* 7th ed. (New Jersey: Prentice Hall, 1996) 43.
[11] W.T. Stace 47.
[12] B.F. Skinner 62.
[13] Clarence Darrow, "An Address Delivered to the Prisoners in the Chicago County Jail," John R. Burr, and Milton Goldinger. *Philosophy and Contemporary Issues.* 7th ed. (New Jersey: Prentice Hall, 1996) 79-87.

Machines and Thought

This discussion is about whether machines can think in a manner akin to that of human beings. Inextricably linked to this is the problem of how much like machines people are. In discussing the question we must examine the various theories which try to account for human behaviour and whether the mind - if it exists - plays a part in that behaviour. We must do this in order to discover the nature of mind for man is essentially thought to consist of mind. If the mind does not exist, then man is only a machine, albeit a complex one.

Why is this question of the possibility of robotic thought and the humanism of machines so important? Because man has traditionally held himself higher than all other animals and if we can create robots that really think, then something of our uniqueness and magic will be lost. Indeed, from a religious point of view also, if it was shown that man himself was just a machine, then the notion that man was specially created in the image of God would seem invalid, and Mary Shelley's notion of man as some kind of inhuman animal would be realized.[1] In addition, if man is all machine and no spirit then what happens to our religious and spiritual beliefs regarding life after death? And what of free will? If man were a machine then would the notion of free will vanish? And if free will were to be proved non-existent then man would not be able to choose his behaviour and would not be morally accountable for his actions.

So is man simply a complex machine? If so, and we can manufacture machines to imitate man's physical and mental processes, would these characteristics then constitute humanness? Would the machine be able to *think* in the conventional sense of the word? In order to answer this we must look at what we mean by "thought."

Thought

Thought is one of the capacities that define us as human beings. Whether you believe man is a machine or not, all depends on whether you insist on man being an entirely physical being or not. It is this which constitutes the mind-body problem.

Materialism maintains that man is physical only.[2] The view that man has a soul is thus invalid. Some theorists equate the soul with the concept of mind; for materialists there is no mind. Death for the materialist philosopher is not death of the soul because there is nothing apart from the physical known as soul. Death is only a termination of the biological and physical processes that make up the complex nervous system.

Let us examine how some of the tenets of materialism affect the man versus machine debate. According to materialism, our knowledge is based on predictability. Everything has a cause and an effect. Man is not the centre of the universe, he is just another organism. All organisms run along physical lines without the need for a soul. Metaphysical notions like mind, consciousness and even ghosts therefore do not exist.

All human-related events therefore, can be reduced to matter and motion. Experience is only a matter of mechanical processes of the brain; this suggests that men are merely biological machines, and therefore robots are equal to men. The behaviour of all organisms is based on reaction to stimuli. This means that behaviour is mechanical, with response to stimuli being a reflexive action.

Let us look in more detail at this from a materialist perspective. The brain is the origin of all behaviour because the brain is the stimulus. Brain activity can be divided into memory, imagination and reason. Actions result from the visualization of a desire of an external object or event. The desire causes the individual to imagine achieving it; this energises the muscles and initiates action. There is no such thing as dualism: mental and bodily phenomena are just two aspects of the same process. The human body is just a very complex machine. All processes are due to the cooperation of physical and chemical forces. There is no spirit guiding our physical behaviour. The mind does not control behaviour, it merely is a bi-product of neural activity. If there were no mind, behaviour would function as normal, because mind is only a system of material processes underlying behaviour.

From this standpoint, men are only automatons. A complex robot if asked whether it had a mind would answer "yes" because the robot's control processes would be like man's: material and physical. Indeed what might cause the robot to answer that it had a mind would not be the possession of a mind, but merely cerebral processes in a material based system.

According to materialism, the human existence is relegated to a level of determinism. Bodily movements are controlled by predetermined laws of physics and chemistry. If the mind equals cerebral conditions, then a particular conscious state equals specific neural functioning. Individual behaviour will therefore be determined and regulated by physico-chemical processes in the brain.

Monism sees the organism as one materialist organic system. There is no need for the problem of deciding when mind suddenly appeared in man's evolutionary history. Man has evolved into a biological machine just like plants or other lesser organisms.

Interactionism on the other hand, says that the expression of human life is more than simply the sum of its parts.[3] An explanation in material terms only, is therefore insufficient. Interactionists hold that materialism relies too much on biology to maintain its tenets. Behaviour is not just a matter of stimulus and response based on biological processes as materialism holds; it is also about the human organism functioning and adapting to the environment with a view to fulfilling its desires. Interactionism does acknowledge the similarity between man and machine, but man has something which a machine does not have: a conative impulse which works in order to fulfil a purpose.

Humans are also influenced by future events; this rules out the mutually exclusive view dictated by a stimulus-response scenario. The way humans can understand meaning through symbols further adds weight to the ineffectiveness of the stimulus-response mechanism in accounting for behaviour. If the S-R only hypothesis were true, individuals would react differently to written instructions, for instance, because they would not have a mind with which to appreciate meaning. But we can understand meaning; therefore mind exists.

We have examined the possibility of whether Robots can think but can they imitate other human behaviour? Robots could in all probability reproduce almost every aspect of the physical behaviour of humans, but whether they could have feelings is doubtful. Robotic machines would, for instance, obtain no pleasurable aesthetic effects from music because they would not have a mind to grasp the overall effect of the unique melody. Music is more than a sum of notes played in succession. Humans can appreciate this; machines cannot. Using exactly the same notes, but in a different sequence, would destroy the pleasurable effect for humans.

In addition there is the subject of consciousness. Machines are not aware of their environment. So, even if a machine was built which could write original music, it would not be aware that it had. Even if it told you it felt the music, it would only be a statement meant to convey the action of feeling, but it would not actually and consciously feel anything. In essence, how could you prove that the machine was conscious of the fact that it had written the music? And if the machine expressed sadness or joy at hearing the music, how would you know that it was expressing genuine feelings, and not merely acting out some artificial mode of behaviour labelled "emotions" which had been previously "fed" to the machine in the form of software?

One ramification of the importance of consciousness is that pleasurable human activities cannot be accounted for simply in S-R terms. The perception of external phenomena involves registering the phenomena through physical-chemical means and combining this with sensory elements to produce a qualitatively different understanding than that capable by a machine, which would lack the sensory processes and thus detract from the machine's ability to comprehend, in a sophisticated manner, its external environment. Therefore the necessary component the machine lacks is "mind." The machine works in a kind of S-R manner: the operator presses a button and the machine operates. In the case of very complex machines, their behaviour would constantly be stimulated by their environment.

A. A. Luce, a metaphysician and idealist, holds the view that we cannot divide the object we sense, the sense data and the unperceivable substance of the material.[4] Therefore, if we agree, it would seem that the materialist theory is invalid. At any rate, the components of human perception work as one whole; machines lack these important perceptual components. Humans are more than biological processors of information. Sensory data requires a mind to interpret it. Sense data cannot be appreciated without mind; it is part of mind.

John Hosper's idea that humans cannot feel another's pain is also relevant to the debate.[5] Even sophisticated Robots would be similar in this respect: just like humans they would not be able to determine the feelings of another living being.

In addition, humans can only prove the existence of another's pain by visual and auditory perception; they can detect behaviour which is a result of pain and respond to it in appropriate ways; and so it would be with complex, robotic machines. The human and machine according to Hosper's tenet both respond to signals: that is the behaviour shown by the person in pain is an indicator of that pain, and the response is based on that indicator.

However, there is a human capacity that robots definitely could not imitate: acting. Humans can readily tell if a person's behaviour is genuine or not, but how could a robot know? After all, a machine would detect the visual signs of a person imitating distress, and would detect auditory signals i.e. crying out, and would consequently, and falsely, assume genuine behaviour on the part of the person acting. And also, in a society of humans and machines, how would a human distinguish between another human and a robot?

Finally, there is the subject of the extinction of human consciousness and the soul. If machines do eventually replace humans, then surely human consciousness and culture, and the literature, the music and the emotions of human love and hate which constitute it, will vanish forever, and no one will be around to lament the loss, save the android witness.

In conclusion, robots we must admit, would be very good at certain specific tasks requiring no emotional interference - like beating world class chess players at chess - but would be useless in areas of activity where feelings and sensitivity come into play. Who can imagine a robot counsellor, for instance, giving comfort to a distressed human patient, and declaring, "Yes, of course, I know how you feel!"

Many philosophers as one would expect, posit the existence of mind and body working together. When humans do physical tasks they use their mind together with their physical body. However, despite the fact that machines do not have a mind, they already control aeroplane flight systems, process information efficiently and solve immensely difficult mathematical problems. Computers - providing they are in perfect working order - also never make mistakes, humans do (although computers could produce errors if one of their electronic circuits were to fail).

The thought processes of humans are also very chaotic with no rules controlling thought operation; the behaviour of computing machines on the other hand, does require rules to control their behaviour. In this sense, if we know the rules governing the robot's programming then we could determine the machine's behaviour; a robotic society would be entirely deterministic and predictable. If we wanted to make machines more human, we would have to introduce a "flaw program" whereby the machine was programmed to make mistakes at certain intervals, but this of course would be an aesthetic adjustment only; it would have no practical use. As the "thought processes" of computers would not be under the machine's control, and as they would be unable to constantly assess their decisions and desires (could machines ever really have desires?), they would need to be given "consciousness software" so that they could question their own behaviour; this would be important not for them but for us, so that we could believe that they were really thinking and therefore alive. And in addition, humans have a constant appetite for knowledge and an ego which needs to be satisfied; machines could use their knowledge to fulfil some specific task but could they ever be enthusiastic about it? And what of morality in machines? They could quite conceivably be able to determine right from wrong, but only because the programmer feeds them with a list of rules and regulations which the machine has been taught to label "good" or "bad" by its creator; but it could never interpret special or original cases not contained in its memory. Machines would in all probability never be able to reproduce these human propensities. The machine lacks mind; and even if we define mind only as a system where external phenomena is represented internally, this would not really constitute mind, merely an aspect of memory. Without consciousness, the machine would simply be an expensive, animated object whose purpose would waver between tool and toy.

Maybe Alan Turing would have been surprised at how little progress we have made with computers bearing in mind his hopes for them at Bletchley Park during the war.[6] However, optimistically speaking, although we can see possible limits to machine intelligence now, we cannot foresee what future improvements in technology might bring and what computers will pass The Turing Test. And what of those really clever machines which succeed in passing the test and convince us of their humanness? Will they really care?

Notes

[1] Mary Shelley, *Frankenstein*, (Hertfordshire: Wordsworth, 1993).
[2] Hugh Elliot, "Materialism," *Philosophy and Contemporary Issues*, ed. John R. Burr and Milton Goldinger, (New Jersey: Prentice Hall, 1996) 391-399.
[3] C.E.M.Joad, "The Mind as Distinct from the Body," *Philosophy and Contemporary Issues*, ed. John R. Burr and Milton Goldinger, (New Jersey: Prentice Hall, 1996) 400-405.
[4] A. A. Luce, *Philosophy and Contemporary Issues*, ed. John R. Burr and Milton Goldinger, (New Jersey: Prentice Hall, 1996) 406-415.
[5] John Hospers, "The Problem of Other Minds," *Philosophy and Contemporary Issues*, ed. John R. Burr and Milton Goldinger, (New Jersey: Prentice Hall, 1996) 416-422.
[6] Christopher Evans, "Can a Machine Think,?" *Philosophy and Contemporary Issues*, ed. John R. Burr and Milton Goldinger, (New Jersey: Prentice Hall, 1996) 431-443.

The Irrelevance of God: Sartre and Ayer

What place will God occupy in the new Utopia? What religion will reign supreme? Let us address these questions by first considering a quote from the great logician, Bertrand Russell:

> I think all the great religions of the world - Buddhism, Hinduism, Christianity, Islam and communism - both untrue and harmful. It is evident as a matter of logic that, since they disagree, not more than one of them can be true. With very few exceptions, the religion which a man accepts is that of the community in which he lives, which makes it obvious that the influence of environment is what has led him to accept the religion in question.[1]

As Russell notes, all the major religions of the world seem to be fighting an unending competition to win men's souls. And as he rightly observes, people tend to choose the religion of their town or country; so for example, an Englishman will choose Christianity rather than Buddhism or Islam, although there are of course many exceptions to this rule, especially as people are travelling to, and living in, countries not of their birth.

Just as the English language appears to be becoming the universal language of trade and science, it is not impossible to rule out the prospect of a universal religion in our new Utopia. But what form will it take? The nearest means of approximating an answer is by looking at the theology of one particular religion which was founded in Japan: "Mahikari."[2] The religion was begun by Kotama Okada (1901-1974) after he supposedly experienced divine revelations from God.

Mahikari, which calls itself a "spiritual organization," appears to have spread slowly around the world and has believers of ninety ethnic groups across seventy-five countries. What is interesting in a egalitarian sort of way about the religion is that it, "...welcomes people of any ideology, nationality, occupation, or faith..."[3] (Of course what religion today professes not to be egalitarian?) There are some peculiar beliefs which form an essential core of the religion, like for example the belief in ancestor worship. Re-incarnation is also an integral part of the religion, as is the idea that whatever affects us adversely in this life is due to the pain we or our relations caused others in a previous one.

One of the achievements of the faith is a magnificent temple building called the "Main World Shrine," which is located in the city of Takayama, Gifu Prefecture, Japan. The elements of its structure seem to have been taken from any typical Japanese shrine; but something modern, perhaps postmodern has been infused into the overall design. If we try to envisage a universal church, a place for people to gather and think about and praise God in the new Utopia, then aesthetically, I can imagine something similar to the Mahikari Main World Shrine.

The most important question to consider however, is will we seek, and will we really need a religious life? If science can cater for all our needs then maybe religion will become redundant. Of our need for the religious life, Bertrand Russell says:

> Religion is based, I think, primarily and mainly upon fear. It is partly the terror of the unknown, and partly the wish to feel that you have a kind of elder brother who will stand by you in all your troubles and disputes. Fear is the basis of the whole thing - fear of the mysterious, fear of defeat, fear of death. Science can help us to get over this craven fear in which mankind has lived for so many generations. Science can teach us, and I think our hearts can teach us, no longer to look round for imaginary supports, no longer to invent allies in the sky, but to look to our own efforts here below to make this

> world a fit place to live in, instead of the sort of place that the churches in all these centuries have made it.[4]

If we can conquer the world and its problems, and more importantly conquer our unrestrained penchant to destroy the landscape and other human beings, then just maybe we will not need God. Perhaps we will really reach the point in the destiny of homo-sapiens when we will really depend on ourselves. We will be alone, terrifyingly so, and whether God exists or not, we shall not need him. We shall not need him to tell us right from wrong in our Utopia; we shall invent our own morality and our own commandments - the commandments of ManGod.

Jean Paul Sartre echoes similar thoughts when he says that God's existence or non-existence has no affect on the fact that man is alone in the world.[5] Whether God exists or not makes no difference to the existentialist point of view.[6] There is no God-given universal rule of morality which can guide man in his actions; no one to tell us what is right and what is wrong; no clear signs to take away the responsibility of freedom. The emphasis is on man (humanism) and not on God.[7] As Sartre says, "...we are now upon the plane where there are only men."[8]

When a man chooses a particular course over another, it is only him who morally labels it good or bad. Man knows he has many possible choices; only the course chosen has any worth. Even not choosing is a choice; there is no escape from freedom. Even if it could be proven that God really existed, there is still no release from the anguish of choice.[9]

Sartre believes that in order to maintain a law-abiding society, moral values are needed; but they exist *a priori*; therefore God is irrelevant.[10] Man is himself responsible for everything he does in society, and when he commits himself to a course of action, he commits not only himself but mankind too.[11] Indeed, Sartre believes that man and not God, generates man.

And how will the irrelevance of God affect the morality of mankind in the new Utopia? For Sartre the central problem is not whether God exists and thereby creates some *a priori* and universal code of morals, but that morality is decided by man himself. Every situation is unique; there is no guide for man to discover the correct moral path. Man must choose himself. He can use his intellect, but he must still choose. Man must invent his own moral law with every choice that he has to make. According to Sartre, if God does not exist, then he cannot invent morals, and if God cannot invent morals then man must. Making sense of morality is a personal thing. Acts cannot be judged by some universal God-given criteria, but only by the person committing them.

Not only Sartre, but A.J. Ayer also questions the nature of morals. Their attack on morality takes different forms and expresses similar *and* different ideas. Ayer's critique of morality is heavily influenced by the Cartesian concept of certainty. That is, the notion of only concerning oneself with founding knowledge on premises that are indubitable. Sartre too acknowledges the Cartesian influence when he says that the *cogito* is "...the absolute truth of consciousness as it attains to itself."[12] Unlike Descartes he rejects the existence of God, yet confuses the issue when he declares that God does not exist but then talks about an "intelligible heaven."[13]

Ayer not only says that we cannot prove that God exists, but also that we cannot prove that he does *not* exist.[14] But why is the existence of God important to morality anyway? Because it limits the origin of a moral code to man rather than to some being who defines universal moral truths. Having established the importance of God to moral matters, Ayer dismisses God through lack of proof: God cannot be accounted for by Ayer's "principal of verification."[15] This principle is an important one and so we will diverge momentarily to explain it.

The principle of verification

According to Ayer's precept, the principle of verification is a scientific yardstick whereby the proposition of a sentence can be validated or nullified. In defining the use of the principle, Ayer believes that every proposition is either true or false. Ayer then acknowledges that certain sentences do not contain propositions, and refrains from using terminology which describes the reputed nature of prepositions that allow a subjective element of analysis to come into play. In avoiding further difficulties arising from the analysis of sentence propositions, Ayer places emphasis on applying his principle of verification directly to the sentence rather than the thing proposed. He also suggests expanding the meaning of "proposition" but then disregards this because it would mean disrupting his criteria of stating explicitly whether a proposition was true or false. Ayer's final solution is to use the term "statement" to refer to any sentence which is valid grammatically and uses "proposition" to describe the expressions of sentences. His principle of verification then, is a method of classifying statements which are associated with the class of propositions and those that are not. Ayer concludes his use of the verification principle by differentiating between "strong" and "weak" verification.[16]

With regard to morality and the verification principle, Ayer himself acknowledges that in a certain sense, the verification principle is insignificant with regard to morality because moral statements which contain words which are used to describe moral sentiment only induce feeling (thus belonging to the unverifiable realm of psychology) and are therefore not informative about truth or falsehood. Indeed the verification principle is *only* significant - with regard to ethics - to the extent that it can be used in situations where a system of values is agreed on beforehand.[17]

At any rate, the result is that one is left with a pessimistic taste in the mouth even if Ayer does not state explicitly the ramification of his view. Pessimism arises because following the denial of God, Ayer offers no step forward, no word of comfort to those seeking it. Sartre, in contrast does: the hope is that despite the non-existence of God, man can be optimistic because he can control his own destiny.[18] But hope is only offered to those who commit themselves to action. There is cold comfort for those who do not succeed in life because it is their own inaction, not circumstances of birth or social position, which determine their fate.[19] To Sartre, every man is an artist; Sartre robs those who paint a meagre self-portrait of any form of consolation.[20]

In Ayer's approach to morality, the whole matter of how to assess moral dilemmas is inextricably linked to the verification principle. Ayer first of all focuses on eliminating those contents of ethics (psychological-dependent moral experience, moral injunctions and contents of a general metaphysical orientation) which cannot be empirically verifiable and are thus of no concern to him, and concentrates on propositions which express definitions of ethical terms. Ethical concepts in themselves are of a pseudo-scientific nature, cannot be verified and thus lie out of the sphere of Ayer's enquiry.

Sartre, on the other hand, tackles the whole problem of morality head on. He does not see the debate of the existence or non-existence of God as the central issue; the key theme of Sartre's diatribe on morality is the complete irrelevance of God in the moral affairs of man. Sartre is a pragmatist; he brings the affairs of a supposed heaven down into the world of men, when, for example, he talks about the angel commanding Abraham to sacrifice his son. Sartre questions everything from the existence of the angel to whether Abraham was really Abraham.[21] Sartre further endorses pragmatism rather than academicism when he talks of basing existentialist tenets on the truth rather than "...upon a collection of fine theories, full of hope but lacking real foundations."[22]

For Sartre, man has freedom irrespective of God. Freedom however, is always used in a negative sense by Sartre when he says for example that "man is doomed to freedom" and uses the ordinarily favourable word *choice* in a similarly pessimistic voice when he speaks of the "anguish of choice."[23]

Freedom and choice then, are not gifts to enhance the beauty and quality of selection when confronted with moral alternatives, but serve to illuminate the hopelessness of the human situation in a world without the assistance of a paternal super being to free us from the pain of deciding our own moral fate. As Sartre points out, "a man cannot escape from the sense of complete and profound responsibility."[24]

And although Ayer is against moral injunctions because they are invalid, Sartre indicates an ideal moral path to follow when he says that everyone "...ought always to ask oneself what would happen if everyone did as one is doing..."[25] Sartre's indirect moral injunctions continue when he asks, "Am I really a man who has the right to act in such a manner that humanity regulates itself by what I do?"[26]

If we compare their sometimes different standpoints we can further see that they have similar views with respect to certain points in their philosophical approaches. For example, with regard to God, one may safely conclude that the probability against the existence of God is acknowledged by them both. However, there are also differences between the two theorists: for example, Sarte is a humanist/subjectivist; that is his philosophy is human centred rather than God centred, and he defines subjectivity as "the freedom of the individual subject."[27] Sartre betrays the notion that one's moral identity is dependent on what others think when he talks about "inter-subjectivity."[28] Indeed, this subjectivism is closely associated with mis-perception and is echoed by Sartre's comments on the interpretation of signs in the anecdote about the Jesuit priest who perceived his lack of success in life as God's will.

In contrast, Ayer is a logical positivist; but Ayer and Sartre's different approaches both have principles to guide them in their treatment of ethics. Ayer's principle is the principle of verifiability; Sartre's first principle is "Man is nothing else but that which he makes of himself."[29] And his second principle relates to freedom: "...freedom [is] the foundation of all values."[30] Sartre's importance of the self clearly becomes apparent. Sartre rejects determinism for the potential - and anguish - of self-determinism. God does not determine man's fate; man determines his own. Each man is responsible for everything he does; there can be no excuses, because choice is the fundamental attribute of mankind.

As much as I agree with Sartre's pragmatic notion of choice and his common sense approach to the individual having the freedom to determine his own fate, I fail to follow his reasoning when he says of man, "...in choosing for himself he chooses for all men."[31] There do seem to be echoes of a socialist nature here and in the following sentences: "...nothing can be better for us unless it is better for all."[32] And also in the following: "Our responsibility is thus much greater than we had supposed, for it concerns mankind as a whole" and "...my action is, in consequence, a commitment on behalf of all mankind."[33] Such statements betray a socialist inclination to moral responsibility, and yet time and time again, Sartre talks about man choosing for himself. How can he reconcile the *collective* and *individual* responsibility? I do acknowledge that there are times when a person chooses a particular course of action and thereby decides the fate of others. For example, those Nazi leaders who ordered the deaths of millions of Jews in the extermination camps decided the fate of two groups of people: those whom they sent to their deaths and those later generations of civilized German citizens who were left with an historical legacy of shame.

However, despite this, Sartre's notion that man is "...a legislator deciding for the whole of mankind..." has a limited number of applications, and it is sometimes hard to find concrete examples to support this idea.[34]

And what about when Sartre says, "...we are unable ever to choose the worst. What we choose is always the better..."[35] Does he really believe that we *always* make the right decision when faced with a number of possible alternatives?

To conclude, both Ayer and Sartre seek the same thing: proof; proof of God, proof of knowledge. Ayer acknowledges that the only proof that he can be certain of relates to the logic of propositions and uses his verification principle to achieve it. He excludes all the preoccupations of a history of philosophers, because any metaphysical knowledge is dubitable. Sartre firmly believes that he will never find any proof when assessing the possible existence of any stimuli that might control man. For Sartre, man still has to use his mental faculties and instinct to decide on the rightness or wrongness of the moral act in each new situation as it comes along. In this respect, Sartre is a realist. In the account of Abraham and the angel, Sartre asks, "Where are the proofs?"[36] For Sartre, there can be no proof with regard to moral correctness; moralism is based on subjectivism: if a man chooses a course of action, it is only him who says it is good. There is no universal morality, no criteria by which man can assess the justice of the moral dilemma. Every man chooses for himself. Each man is faced with the anguish and uncertainty of different courses of action; and only the course chosen, the one that decides one's happiness or misery, is the course that has value for the individual. But the reader of Sartre is faced with a dilemma here: does one allow oneself to be lured by Sartre's instinctualism, as when he talks about his pupil being faced with different and hard alternatives and then using his intuition to decide his future actions, or does one accept Sartre's token acknowledgement that there *are* values of a universal nature, as for example when he talks about honesty as an a priori, mandatory construct and posits the existence of values?

Sartre's conclusion that man must, as a result of no universal moral code, decide in every situation what he must do, is for me, the most stimulating premise. As he says, "...nothing remains but to trust in our instincts..."[37]

Ayer, on the other hand, is anti-subjectivist and puts forward arguments against holding such a view. He insists on a moral criteria; a consensus of opinion regarding moral acts: "In short, we find that argument is possible on moral questions only if some system of values is presupposed."[38] Ayer however, generally concerns himself with linguistic veracity because it is the only thing he can really be certain of. He dispenses with metaphysics. Ayer is only interested in the logic of propositions of sentences. The fact that he chooses to investigate only the truth of sentences stems from his belief that this type of data is the only truth that can be known. Ayer's arguments thus seem justifiably strong because he limits himself to what he can know only with certainty, although he fails to convince because of the limits of application of the tenets he puts forward.

Sartre's truth is that there is no God; man is alone and doomed to freedom. Indeed, Sartre's basic existential tenet is that man is only what he makes himself; man is his own future. For me, this is appealing because if man can choose what he will become, then it is an optimistic philosophy because it implies hope. However, it also presupposes that if man gets himself into incurable difficulties then no one is there to help him - a terrifying prospect.

For many people like myself, the admission that we readily blame others, personal circumstances, and fate in general for life's misfortunes rather than our own lack of action, instinctively weakens determinist arguments. I am inclined to feel persuaded by Sartre's moral philosophy rather more than Ayer's primarily because of Sartre's pragmatic and accessible explication of the freedom of choice; he puts forward some lucid and provocative arguments concerning this. I feel that if the freedom to choose is an illusion, part of a pre-ordained trick, and I counteract the effects by not choosing, then as Sartre says, "...that is still a choice."[39]

Ayer's tenet asserts only the efficaciousness of the verification principle in determining truth, but it is not an all encompassing truth, only a marginal, linguistic one. So in this sense the application of Ayer's philosophical principles cannot be applied to a plethora of moral and other philosophical problems and therefore, for me, is rendered less accessible. This in itself is not the fault of Ayer but simply an inherent attribute of a system of investigation which is relatively successful when confined to the narrow parameters of linguistic curiosities.

Notes

[1] Bertrand Russell, *Russell's Best: Silhouettes in Satire*, (Routledge: New York, 1995) 53.
[2] Dr. Andris K. Tebecis, *Mahikari*, (Yoko Shuppan: Tokyo, 1982).
[3] *Sukyo Mahikari: The Main World Shrine*, ([Gifu]): Sukyo Mahikari, Gifu],n.d.).
[4] Russell 49.
[5] Jean Paul Sartre, "Existentialism as a Humanism," Kaufmann, Walter. *Existentialism from Dostoevsky to Sartre*, (New York: Meridian, 1989) 369.

[6] Sartre 369.
[7] Sartre 368.
[8] Sartre 353.
[9] Sartre 352.
[10] Sartre 352-3.
[11] Sartre 350.
[12] Sartre 361.
[13] Sartre 353.
[14] Alfred Jules Ayer. *Language Truth and Logic.* (New York: Dover Publications, inc., 1952) 114-15.
[15] Ayer 5.
[16] Ayer 5-16.
[17] Ayer 22, 105, 107-8.
[18] Sartre 347.
[19] Sartre 353.
[20] Sartre 359, 364.
[21] Sartre 351.
[22] Sartre 360.
[23] Sartre 351-2, 353, 357.
[24] Sartre 351.
[25] Sartre 351.
[26] Sartre 352.
[27] Sartre 350.
[28] Sartre 361.
[29] Sartre 349.
[30] Sartre 366.
[31] Sartre 350.
[32] Sartre 350.
[33] Sartre 350.
[34] Sartre 351.
[35] Sartre 350.
[36] Sartre 351.
[37] Sartre 355.
[38] Ayer 111.
[39] Sartre 363.

www.ingramcontent.com/pod-product-compliance
Ingram Content Group UK Ltd.
Pitfield, Milton Keynes, MK11 3LW, UK
UKHW040601210726
13854UKWH00008B/1708

9 781906 801700